SEEDS
WONDER OF
BORNEO

SEEDS WONDER OF BORNEO

LOJI ROJI SAIBI

PARTRIDGE
A Penguin Random House Company

To order additional copies of this book, contact
Toll Free 800 101 2657 (Singapore)
Toll Free 1 800 81 7340 (Malaysia)
orders.singapore@partridgepublishing.com

www.partridgepublishing.com/singapore

For my wife and children
'To love and be loved'

CHAPTER 1

Why do some people live longer than others? Even as a child, I was fascinated by that question. Maybe it's because I was born on Borneo, the world's third largest island and home to one of the oldest rainforests on earth. It has long been thought that plants and seeds in the rainforest might hold the secret to prolonging human life. I would be given a chance to prove that true.

Rainforests once almost entirely covered this island. It's worth noting that the forest is so rich in plant and animal life that every year previously unknown species are discovered. Such biodiversity is not only rare but also endangered.

Since the time I grew up on the Malaysian end of the island, Borneo's landscape has changed tremendously. As reported by the *Vancouver Sun* on 10 January 2015, researchers from the Carnegie Institute of Science, using satellite images, concluded that up to 80 per cent of the rainforest on Borneo, especially in the two states of Sabah and Sarawak, had been destroyed or degraded in the past thirty years by legal and illegal logging and now palm-oil production. It was also noted that less than 10 per cent of the primary forest remained.

This was bad news for the indigenous inhabitants. They were the last hunter-gatherers in South East Asia. It had become impossible for them to remain nomads and carry on their traditional lifestyle, as their habitat had been destroyed.

The World Music Rainforest Festival was an annual event depicting the lives of the rainforest people on the island of Borneo. It was attended by researchers from all over the world. I had recently retired from government service, and as the festival date approached, I was busy answering calls from friends in China, Japan, Australia, Germany, the United Kingdom, and the United States who were all planning to visit and in need of my assistance.

Professor Wong Chung Huat came from China for the festival. When I met him at the airport, he was a bit reserved and didn't say much. I put him in a taxi to his hotel and remained at the airport to pick up a friend from Japan. I met Professor Wong in the hotel lobby later, and he had so much to talk about, there seemed to be no stopping him.

Professor Wong was a research fellow at Peking University in Beijing, dealing with herbs from roots and trees. He had made some breakthroughs, especially on the potential of some roots and plants for improving human wellness.

'How are you doing now, Mr Zaidi?' Professor Wong asked. We had been communicating on social media since meeting at the previous year's festival.

'Doing well, Professor, as now I am a retiree,' I replied.

'I am really fascinated by what I see around your city,' he said when we had settled ourselves at the sofa table, having our drinks.

'What is it that really attracts you, Professor?' I asked.

He was so excited when he told me what he had seen along the route from the airport to the hotel. 'The green areas your people have maintained all over the place, really fascinating!' he enthused.

'You should go to the rural areas, Professor, to see more of our forest and its contents.' I encouraged him to venture further and to see more of what our rainforest could offer. The forest was well known for the biodiversity of its flora and fauna, including different species of animals, birds, fish, and other wildlife.

'Yeah, that is what I want to do, starting now. I intend to go deep into your forests and do research,' he said in a serious manner. After being involved in research in the field of botany for a long time, he had become an activist with the NGOs in China, trying to save the forests in his country as well as the tropical rainforest.

'That's great, Professor. You should go ahead and do what you intend. Our forests may not last long for such a purpose,' I told him. I knew our forests had been gradually depleted.

'Is that so? Why?' he asked in quiet manner. He was a bit surprised to hear that our forests were no longer what they used to be. He knew the rainforest was being depleted but not to what extent.

'I will tell you later, Professor. We meet again at the festival site tonight, right?' I asked as we concluded our meeting. I had to go to see my friend from Japan.

The World Music Rainforest Festival was held every year at the cultural village in Kuching, Sarawak. The village was a representation of indigenous dwelling houses depicting indigenous people's living conditions and lifestyle. World and indigenous musicians came from all over the globe to participate in this unique event. The festival was well attended each year by music enthusiasts as well as those who did work related to the rainforest.

That evening, the professor and I met again at the cultural village, a showpiece for outsiders on the culture, nature, and adventures that were unique to the natives. Each house was built to represent an ethnic group. In each of these houses was placed the group's handicrafts, and a local musician would play ethnic music for the visitors. There was also a cultural performance at a theatre located in a building at the centre of the village.

We went to watch a show that portrayed – through music and songs – the life of the indigenous people called the Dayaks, which consisted of several ethnic groups. I attended the cultural programme with the professor and became engrossed in the music of the indigenous groups. Though we continued to talk about his work, we could still appreciate the programme being presented.

A stringed musical instrument called a *sape* played by the local indigenous group had a very unique sound. It was quite similar to the Indian sitar, but the tone was more localised, reflecting the sounds and rhythm of the local surroundings. These natives lived in longhouses along the river banks. Some of them lived in the valleys and hills of the interior. Listening to the melody carried me back to an experience I'd had in a rural area of the country.

I was involved in an educational project undertaken by an NGO. The flight from the state capital to the northern region stopped over at an airport in another city in the north. From there, our group took a smaller plane to a small town. The group was sponsored by a logging company as part of its social corporate responsibility to the indigenous people.

We were to carry out an educational programme to help the people adjust to more settled lives. The target group was those who had been moving from one place to another like nomads. The government had just started a development project for them.

After half an hour, we arrived at our destination. Since it was almost six o'clock in the evening, we decided to settle for a night at the local hotel, Seri Malaysia.

The next morning, we proceeded to the project site using four-wheel drive. The journey involved following a winding and tortuous road left by the logging company. The vehicles had to cross small rivers, climb hilly terrain, and even be pushed once in the while when stuck on the muddy path.

It took us seven hours to arrive at the small village of indigenous folks called Batu Bala. They were living in makeshift shelters scattered all over the place. They had been encouraged to settle on small plots of land, where they did slash-and-burn farming, moving on once the land was depleted.

The educational project undertaken by our group was to involve adults and children in the community. Our group consisted of teachers, local representatives, and NGO workers. The community was still far behind in terms of basic development compared to those in the urban areas.

According to the person in charge, Ismail Razak, the project had been implemented a few months earlier. He had been appointed by the local NGO, HELP US, to spearhead the educational programme. Being a local person, he was familiar with the community and was readily accepted by the indigenous group.

'The school project is well received by the community. The children are keen to learn, and they learn fast,' he'd explained when he briefed us the night before. The group also provided other forms of assistance, such as helping the men learn carpentry work and the women the art of weaving. The goal was to provide aid for the needy by attending to short-term basic needs and empowering the natives to be self-sufficient in the long run.

'The cost of the project is quite substantial, and because of that, the team can only go to the site two or three times during the project implementation,' he said.

When asked what would happen when the project was complete, he said, 'The committee at the village level will help monitor it.' The committee consisted of community members selected by the villagers. They were to oversee project implementation and monitor progress and follow-up.

Ismail related the challenges that arose when they first started the programme. They had to organise get-togethers with the elders who were not keen for the children to know about modern things. They believed that once these young ones were exposed to the new and weird things, they would be influenced to do something against their community norms.

The villagers still held steadfastly to their customs and daily practices, which had been passed down from their ancestors. The norms, including the way of life in the community, had to be adhered to by the villagers.

In one of the get-togethers, there were a lot of arguments, and the villagers even wanted the project team to go back. However, a government officer who was also present told them what the programme would be about. The villagers were convinced that it would not disrupt their norms and ways. Thus, the project could proceed.

Ismail was confident that the children of the community would benefit from the implementation of the project. The team was well prepared in that they were willing to be more flexible with the programme. They were sensitive to the community they were dealing with. I was once an educator and now I was interested in rainforest research, so I was invited to join the group as an observer. My interest in indigenous people and the controversy regarding the depletion of the rainforest became a passion.

Historically, the indigenous people of Sarawak were encouraged to settle down during the colonial era in the mid-twentieth century. But some of them decided to remain nomadic and carry on their traditional lifestyle. These people had a unique, ancient lifestyle, with sago (a starch) as their staple food. Sago was extracted from palm trees called *mulong* in the local dialect. Sago flour is now popularly used in baking cakes.

These people also relied on hunting wild boar or deer and fishing. They roamed the forest and jungle in search of animals. They lived in the forest and used the resources at their disposal. The forest and jungle to them were heaven on earth where they were free to do as they pleased.

Before going for the performance at the theatre, Professor Wong and I had visited some of the indigenous dwelling houses in the cultural village. We went from one house to another. 'This is really fantastic. We can see for ourselves the lives these people have,' Professor Wong commented.

'Indeed, that's the reason the cultural village was built,' I said.

'A very good move by the authority,' Professor Wong replied. 'At least, for those who have no time to visit the actual village in the interior, they could get a first impression here.' As we walked along the path between the houses, there were certain parts of the village covered by trees and bushes, representing the forests in the country. When I looked at the little forest in the cultural village, my mind began to wander to the fate of our rainforest.

The rainforest itself as a whole had been affected greatly by physical development throughout the country. Logging, palm-oil plantations, and hydroelectric dams were destroying the indigenous peoples' habitat and traditional way of life. This development also disturbed the well-being of the orangutans, pygmy elephants, and sun bears.

There should be a concerted effort from various sectors to save this paradise from disappearing from the face of the earth. The effort must be genuine and embrace even the international community. The local authorities may not be able to do what is expected of them due to political interference.

Was there still hope to save the rainforest for the indigenous people in particular and the world in general? The indigenous people in the upper part of the northern region had been fighting for their rights for a long time. Although they could not possibly go against the might of the authorities, their resistance against the illegal destruction of the forest did save some pristine areas. In fact, the community was glad it could defend and protect the traditional territory of its ancestors on one of the rivers, which remained a wonderful oasis in the virgin forest.

'What has the state done to preserve the forest?' Professor Wong asked when he was also attracted by the little forest in the cultural village.

'They have implemented some kind of replanting project and turned some areas into natural parks,' I told him.

'But that won't help much if they don't stop the activity by the logging companies,' he continued. That was precisely what had led to the indigenous people protesting against the illegal logging and deforestation. Their resistance to the act of deforestation by some irresponsible parties had in fact achieved some success.

The people wanted to take their future into their own hands. They went in against all odds to protect their ancestral heritage and culture. They organised systematic blockades of logging roads. They went to the capital cities to protest so that the authorities would listen to their plea. Some of their NGOs went overseas to spread their grievances. With persistent effort from the indigenous people and the support of the international community, I had no doubt that there was still hope to save the rainforest.

When the performance in the cultural village came to its climax, I was awakened from my nostalgic mode by the loud shouting voice of the native warrior as he jumped into the air, accompanied by the beat of a drum. Professor Wong, who was sitting next to me in the packed theatre, was shaken with surprise when the native warrior aimed a blowpipe at him. The native warrior, full of energy to be doing a dance onstage in front of an audience, shot the balloon hanging above our heads. Bang! This was followed by tumultuous applause; the audience was really impressed by the native warrior's performance. That also ended the show.

CHAPTER 2

As we left the cultural village, Professor Wong was still very much interested in knowing more about the forests. We continued our conversation at the Damai Resort Hotel nearby, where he was staying.

Professor Wong observed, 'You must be sad, knowing that the forests are gradually disappearing.'

'I was born and brought up in the rural area,' I told him, 'so I feel sad to see our virgin forests being destroyed. But the fact remains that when the authorities are not firm enough in dealing with the culprits, the problem persists.'

I knew how hard it was to change from what we used to be into something entirely different. The authorities wanted the indigenous groups to accept changes brought about by the clearing of forests for plantations and other things. Logging activity was encouraged by the authorities to generate income for the country. This saddened those who were born and brought up in those surroundings, including me.

I was born and grew up in a rural village of a few hundred people. When I was small, all around me were forests and trees. We relied on the forest for most of our existence. We used the trees to build our houses and bridges. Tree trunks and branches were used to cook and trap animals.

My father was once employed by the timber company. He was the leader of a group of lumberjacks. They worked as loggers to cut trees for local use, such as making furniture and houses. They earned a living and thus could feed their children. However, they were careful not to cut the trees illegally so that the forest remained intact.

The rivers provided us with water all the year round, as well as fish, crabs, clamps, and other waterborne foods. Of course, rivers were also the living places for amphibians and reptiles.

I vividly remembered playing by the river as a child. When the river was at low tide, we played on the extended riverbank like the kids now play with their skateboards. Our skateboards were just pieces of wood. We were never afraid of anything, not even the crocodiles that lurked in the river. We were not even afraid of stonefish living underneath the soft soil along the riverbank – although if we were not careful and stepped on one, it could be painful for our feet. We just enjoyed the moment as we played from morning to evening, especially during school holidays.

The river where we played and took our baths, Sungai Rajang, was the longest in the country. It flowed from up in the mountains. The area at the upper end was mostly covered by thick jungle, with thousands of species of trees. The water was crystal clear. We could easily see fish and prawns under the water, going about their business as if there was nothing bothering them.

But all these were now gone. The rivers were polluted and their banks eroded. There were hardly any waterborne creatures like there had been before. The natives had to make do with whatever they could find or cling to for survival.

Many of the animals who had lived in the forests were no longer there. They had to find some place far away in the deep jungle. This led to hunters being unable to find animals for their hunt. Gone were the days when you just went out to the forest area and made your catch.

One of the educated indigenous activists, Mutang Laso, used to mourn this sad fact. 'Gone are the days when I spent most of my childhood in the forest, which we regarded as a playground. My friends and I would collect honey from the tree trunks and ground fruits and nuts from the forest floor. We'd climb up vines and fruit trees to feed our hungry stomachs.'

He continued, 'We were born and grew up surrounded by mountains. The forest was our only world, and under the dark canopy where the noonday seems like dusk, only the calls of birds and cicadas told us the time of day.' He was really sad to know that this beautiful and pristine forest could now hardly be seen.

Some people said, 'Why look at the past when it gives you only painful memories?' But there was nothing to look at now, and nothing in the future either.

'Your forests have so much to offer to the world,' Professor Wong pointed out. 'There is hardly any researched literature on the contents of your rainforest until now.' He had already travelled to the other countries in the region and conducted research on the herbs and plants. But there was so much to do, as the species were many.

'I am now also quite keen to know more about the potential of these plants, Professor.' I told him what I had experienced as a person who came from an area that relied on the forests.

'I hope your virgin forests can be conserved and sustained for the benefit of all those interested all over the world,' he said.

I totally agreed with him, as I realised the depletion of the forests affected not only the indigenous people but everyone the world over.

As we continued our conversation, I reflected upon what had happened to the indigenous people where we had launched our educational project. They were still to some extent living in an area covered by virgin forest. The community was short of basic necessities, as they had been wandering people previously. The government wanted them to settle down and live like the other communities. They were trying to adapt themselves to a new way of life. But since they had been nomadic from time immemorial, they found it difficult to adapt to such settled lives.

One of the indigenous folks who went to school and continued with his studies until he became a lecturer at the local university used to reminisce about his good old days in the village. 'What we treasured as our assets and heritage are gone now!' he said. He used to enjoy collecting fruits and edible plants, as they grew nonstop all year round. He went hunting, searching for birds and squirrels without difficulty, as they were plentiful. 'The destruction as a result of incessant and indiscriminate logging has left the forest almost inexistent,' he said.

The new generation may not appreciate the treasures of the past. The older generation experienced a life full of serenity and ambience. There was green everywhere, and the river was full of fish and other waterborne foods we could get without difficulty. Life was easy-going, and people were content and happy, although they didn't have much wealth.

It was almost midnight when our conversation came to an end. 'It was really nice to meet you again, Professor Wong,' I said before we bade each other goodnight.

'I am also pleased to be able to meet you this time around, Mr Zaidi,' Professor Wong said.

'I will no doubt remember what you told me about your research on a group of people who lived longer than the others,' I said on a serious note. He had done some research in China regarding the longevity of a certain community. I was fascinated by such rare findings and decided to discover why and how they could live such lives. I remembered Professor Wong's conversation on herbs and plants for wellness and the breakthroughs he had described. There could be more than just herbs and plants involved. How about the seeds of plants?

'Well, goodnight my friend. I will see you some other time.' Professor Wong extended his hand to me.

'Goodnight, Professor. Indeed, we will see each other again on another occasion.' I shook his hand before we parted.

CHAPTER 3

My earnest interest in and commitment to searching for the answer to the question of why some people live longer than others started in Australia, where I was studying and doing much of my research. Natural science subjects attracted me a great deal, mainly due to my background and birthplace.

I started working in my teens, just after I earned a certificate in teaching from the teacher's college. My first posting as a trained non-graduate teacher was in a rural area. Although I was still young and not very experienced, I was respected by my colleagues and students. My studious nature and constant need to keep learning made me a role model for other young teachers. However, I still felt that I had not done enough to upgrade myself. I went back to school to further my studies and obtain a degree.

As I was fascinated with the tropical rainforest, which was still intact and covering most of my birthplace, I decided to work with the Forest Department. That's how I was given the chance to further my studies in the area of reforestation sustainability.

I was on a study scholarship to pursue a research degree on sustainable forest management. The government would then use my expertise to implement a reforestation programme in my country. This was following a lot of criticisms by NGOs regarding the depletion of the tropical rainforest owing to logging and land-clearing activities.

The issue had come to the attention of the United Kingdom, the United States, and some European countries. In actual fact, some of the agencies from these countries were monitoring the situation in my country. I was working for one of them as a research fellow now. I had retired from full employment with the government several years earlier and was engaged full-time as a research fellow.

Nevertheless, I felt like I was never good at anything. Deep inside, I felt like I had not done anything really substantial for my community. Even now, already retired after working so many years with the government, I still considered myself not as good I would have liked to be. This thought bothered me.

Others on the research team regarded me as someone who was not only knowledgeable but also wise. They had seen how I conducted myself as the person in charge of the overall research project we had undertaken together. They had given me high respect compared to the other leaders of the groups. Some of them, when they greeted me, would call me 'professor', as if I was qualified for that esteemed title.

My interest in research regarding why some people lived longer than others continued. There was a study on how to maintain healthy and purposeful living. The researchers looked at how certain groups of people in certain countries used herbs and plants. These people were able to live longer than others. The research changed my perspective on life and living it well and with a purpose. It led to my pursuit of real research work on the longevity of life on the ground.

At the same time, there was already a body of research on natural resources for health and wellness. These natural resources could be used to produce supplements for fitness and a healthy lifestyle. There were some products already on the market – distributed by well-known names such as Amway, Herbalife, Shaklee, and others – that were in great demand.

However, these products were mainly manufactured using conventional methods, and the effects seemingly were not lasting. The quest for health products that could prolong human life became my passion. This was partly because the demand for health supplements was great, and thus I was encouraged to search for better products. Moreover, I was one of those who took supplements on a regular basis.

Although still studying as required by the Forest Department, I spent most of my time reading the literature on longevity research. I came across an old story being told and retold – that in certain parts of the globe, there were people who lived much longer than the rest. This story made me think that there must be some natural ingredient that could extend our lives. What was this natural source? Could it be the food these people ate, the way they lived, or a supplementary substance of sorts? These questions were always on my mind.

I came to know Professor John Howard, who was involved in food technology research at the university where I was studying in Brisbane, Australia. We often discussed matters of common interest. I was doing some research in the library one day when he came in and saw me.

'How are you today, Mr Zaidi?' said Professor Howard. We had met for the first time when I was a volunteer in the

International Students Department. He had a great interest in my country and its tropical rainforest.

'Not really that good, Professor. Still doing my thesis-writing after the data analysis and a bit exhausted,' I said.

'Why? I thought you had found a formula for fit and well living already!' he said in jest.

'No, Prof, not yet. Still in search of the natural formula. Hoping to find it soon,' I said.

The professor, who was from the department of neuroscience and food technology, used to present papers regarding health and wellness. We would always have a discussion regarding how to stay healthy and fit. He was also involved with longevity research on certain groups of communities in China, Japan, and Europe.

'Do you have any lead on the longevity issue?' I asked as we continued our conversation.

'There are some documents on ancient practices by the natives on some islands in the South East Asia region,' he said.

'Yeah, do you have the documents? Can I have them?' I asked. Professor Howard and I had shared a great relationship right from the start, which made it easy for me to be frank with him.

'Of course. These documents are important for this type of study.' He took a pile of papers from one of his bags and passed it to me.

'Thank you, Prof,' I said.

'You can keep all those. Now I have to go for a meeting with the vice chancellor. See you later,' he said as he left me with the documents in my hands.

The documents contained a lot of information on traditional medicines that were made as well as used by the natives. Aloe Vera leaves were used to heal burns, wounds, and other skin ailments. Arnica plants could be used as an anti-inflammatory and for osteoarthritis. Cranberry was used for urinary disorders, diarrhoea, diabetes, and stomach ailments. The popular ginkgo-leaf extract was used to treat asthma, bronchitis, and fatigue. Another popular item, ginseng root, had been used as medicine, especially in Asia, for over two thousand years. The list went on.

There was also research done by nature lovers who had discovered that certain plants could help prolong human life. I was happy to be in possession of the documents and was engrossed in them most of the time.

Often while studying the documents in the library, I got the feeling that I was being watched by someone. He looked smart in his jacket and necktie, like a familiar film star, Jason Statham. I had seen this fellow following me around for a while. Could he have been instructed to monitor my movements since I came to Australia to further my studies? Was he from one of the agencies involved in saving the rainforest? I was not connected with any interest groups, so I ignored the possibility of being the target of such espionage work.

I completed my research and earned my doctorate. Now I was waiting for my ticket from my sponsor to go back home. It was a Sunday morning. While walking at the riverfront of the city, I met Professor Howard and the man who had been following me all this while.

'Hi there! How are you today, Mr Zaidi?' Professor Howard greeted me.

'Hey, Prof. I am all right; a bit relaxed this time. I have done my thesis submission, and I'm just waiting to go back home,' I explained.

'Great. So you are to continue working with your government?' he asked.

'Sure. But just for a few more years. I'll retire at the age of 56.'

'Good. If that is the case, if you are interested, I recommend that you work with the foundation in the United States,' he said. He was working on a partnership basis with the World Human Life Foundation. The university was sometimes paid by the foundation to conduct projects.

'What is the work about?' I asked.

'It has something to do with what you're passionate about: the search for a product that prolongs human life,' he said.

'How am I to communicate with the foundation?' I asked.

'Well, let me introduce to you Mr Thomas. He is searching for people who have good credentials to work with the foundation,' Professor Howard explained.

'Hey, I am Mr Thomas,' the man introduced himself.

'That would be great, if I could be given the opportunity to work with such a well-known agency,' I said. I had been told about the foundation and its research activity on living a longer life by Professor Howard.

'Well, if you are interested, I will let Mr Thomas arrange a session with you for the recruitment exercise,' Professor Howard suggested.

'Thank you, Prof, and thanks, Mr Thomas,' I said finally. They left me, and I was a bit excited by the new development.

A few days later, I was called by Mr Thomas to meet him at his office at the city centre. His office was quite small in size, and he worked with only a clerk to help him.

'Hey, good morning, Mr Zaidi,' he greeted me as I entered the room.

'Good morning, Mr Thomas,' I answered.

'Please be seated. How are you today?' he asked.

'Fine! I am quite free now. So a bit more relaxed,' I told him.

There was a moment of silence. He looked at me directly and must have been trying to figure out what to say next.

'First,' he began, 'I have to apologize for following you around while you were studying in Australia.'

'I had a hunch that someone was following me when I was on campus,' I said.

'That's right. I was instructed to follow you and gather information about your country's issues regarding its tropical rainforests,' he explained. He really wanted to meet someone who could give him first-hand information on the issue. All he had been able to learn was from social media, and that information may not have painted an accurate picture.

'I see. I was not very concerned about being followed, because I know that I have nothing to hide,' I said.

'I found out about you through Professor Howard. In fact, I wanted to meet you earlier to find out more about the tropical rainforest issue. But couldn't do that due to work pressure,' he explained.

'Well, I am not well versed on the issue. I was sent here to do research on how to sustain forest growth, not so much regarding the problem at home,' I told him. The issue at home attracting so much attention was the destruction of indigenous lifestyles and habitats. I was not fully aware of the issue, as most of the time I had been abroad doing my studies.

'All right. Let's just talk about the foundation's job first,' he said. 'The foundation is based in New York. Its primary business objective is research on how to prolong human living.'

'Where have they done their research?' I asked.

'They have done a lot of research around the globe,' he answered.

'Have they come up with what they are researching about?' I asked.

'So far, they have not come up with a finding regarding a solution for a product or formula,' he explained.

'What do they intend to do?' I asked.

'They are now in the process of pursuing a new lead for ingredients that could be processed into supplements,' he explained.

'Is that why they are recruiting new staff?' I asked.

'Yeah, I was given the job of searching for new staff, in particular a research fellow with credentials,' he said.

'That sounds great! Given the chance, I am interested in joining the research team,' I said.

'Good. I will list you in and let the panel at headquarters decide,' Mr Thomas said.

I informed him that I could only take up the new job when I retired from government service. Before we closed the discussion on the job matter, I asked Mr Thomas whether I could bring along my wife.

'That's all right. If you want her to work with the foundation, I could include her on the list. Could I have her name, please?' Mr Thomas asked.

'Zarrah Nur. She was once a lab assistant at a private local college,' I said.

'All right. She could work as a lab assistant in the research station,' Mr Thomas said.

We then talked about things in general, especially what he had been doing in Australia. I told him about my work as a teacher and then with the Forest Department as a forest officer. Before I left the office, he informed me that the foundation headquarters would contact me to pursue the recruitment.

I was back in my country soon after. I continued doing my work and at the same time helping the government on the reforestation programme until I retired. While waiting for the foundation to make a decision regarding the fellowship appointment, I worked in Singapore with a private enterprise on marketing research products. The company was mainly doing research on technological products for consumers in the country as well as abroad.

Then, one day, I was contacted by the World Human Life Foundation to confirm that I had been appointed as a research fellow and would be working with the research team. They were making arrangements for the research team to be sent to a certain location on the island of Borneo, located between Malaysia and Indonesia.

The research team would mainly process ingredients into supplements. The ingredients to be obtained from the jungle were certain seeds of plants. The research team consisted of a number of scientists in specific fields dealing with plants, seeds, and herbs. I would be given the task of leading the team.

The infrastructure of the project would be designed by the foundation. They were to build a research station in the jungle where the local resources to make the supplement were found. The station would be equipped with all the necessary facilities – administration building, CEO residence, staff quarters, and processing laboratories.

The research team would produce the supplement to be exported around the globe. The station occupied an area of about 150 hectares. The land had been obtained from the local owner from a village some distance away from the area.

It was a big enterprise, and the foundation had spent millions of dollars on the project. Construction had already been started and was almost complete.

We were required to go there once the station was fully constructed. However, as the foundation didn't want to waste much time, they did the recruitment of staff beforehand. The research team was the last group to be sent to the station.

CHAPTER 4

The team boarded a ship from Singapore that took us to the island of Borneo, where the station was located. As we approached the island, we could see it was all covered by forest. It was very beautiful and enchanting. My wife especially was thrilled as we enjoyed the panoramic view of the island from the ship.

The ship got closer to the beach area, and we then used boats to go to the beach, as there were no ports or harbours for a ship on the island. Near where we landed, there was a small fishing village. The people were mostly fishermen and relied on the sea for their livelihood.

The island was occupied by natives, with their villages scattered. However, the interior was mainly unexplored because of the thick forest and jungle. The group went straight to the research station, which was located forty-nine kilometres from the beach.

The dense tropical rainforest and thick jungle looked like heaven to the researchers and nature lovers. The jungle was among the oldest in the region. It contained a lot of materials for research, especially in the field of natural sciences. Flora and fauna of different kinds were present in abundance. Animals and jungle inhabitants were to be found everywhere.

For a long while, explorers had come to the island to hunt animals. Thus the island had become well-known throughout the region. Recently, international corporations like the foundation had started researching the flora and fauna.

The long walk through the jungle took us several hours. The jungle track was full of trees, some tall and huge. It was virgin jungle, and we met several wild animals on the way. But, as we went in a group, the animals ran away as we passed by.

We came across an area where there were fruit trees. Some of the group members and the workers picked and ate the fruits, which were like rambutans. We also met villagers who came to the jungle to obtain logs for making their houses. By the time we arrived at the research station, everybody looked tired.

'Let us have a good rest tonight. It has been a long journey,' Ali Mat said. He was the leader of the project team and in charge of administration. The main team members were fifty, consisting of specialists in botany, agro-science, natural science, and data analysis. The rest were general workers.

'Are we going to start working tomorrow?' Lamin Lamat asked. He was one of the leaders of the group.

'Of course. We need to start our work, and the sooner the better,' the project team leader reminded everybody.

'All right then, everybody take a good rest. Until we meet again tomorrow,' Lamin said to everyone.

My wife and I went to the quarters for our group. There were ten of us in all. We were quite close to each other after having worked together before on several research projects.

Since I was the oldest, they respected me. They allowed my wife and I to stay in one of the rooms by ourselves.

After we unpacked our things, everybody got busy preparing food for dinner. Since most of the team members were Asian, rice was the main menu item. There were also vegetables, fish, and meat. The team members were hungry after the long walk, and so they ate a lot and soon felt sleepy. They went right to bed.

After dinner, I went around the compound by myself. This was my usual way of making sure that after taking food, I would do some walking. While walking, I was in deep thought about what I had gone through in life.

There were five groups that made up the project team, with eighty people in total. These consisted of scientists, analysts, specialists, and some officials of the World Human Life Foundation. I was in charge of the research project, while the administration part was under the project team leader.

'How old were you when you were sent to school?' Lamin inquired while we sat on the veranda after my walkabout.

'I am not sure. In fact, I have never known my real age,' I confessed. Children in my time were seldom registered when they were born, especially among the villagers. Ages were only later registered for the purpose of schooling. I was no exception.

'Didn't your father tell you your age?' Lamin insisted.

'No, not at all. We seldom talked about family matters, or even matters in general,' I said earnestly.

'Never! Why? Your father was quite known by the villagers,' Lamin reminded me. He knew a bit about my family background. He was my countryman.

'I'm not really sure about why. My father liked to keep things to himself,' I explained.

'Possibly you could be somebody one day. Then the world will know all about you,' Lamin consoled me.

'Possibly! Anything is possible in life,' I counselled myself quietly.

Lamin and I would spend quite some time at that research station deep in the island jungle. The project, funded by the International Human Life Sustainability Trust from the World Human Life Foundation in New York, was designed to ascertain whether natural materials such as herbs, seedlings, roots, leaves, and the bark of certain trees could be used to prolong human life. At present, there were numerous supplements using fruits, leaves, roots, and tree bark on sale for the purpose of health and wellness. However, research was still going on to find a more effective form of health supplement that could extend human life and older age.

The station was self-contained, with all the technology required for the research. The laboratories were well equipped. Each laboratory was assigned to do a specific task: processing, quality control, packaging, delivery, and so on.

Life at the station went on as usual. At the quarters near ours, the collection team members were discussing their next task: collecting the seeds, which were the basic research materials. The earlier collection had been exhausted.

'The seeds you are collecting – are there any more in the forest?' Ali asked.

'There could be a lot more, deep inside the jungle,' replied Mohamad Johan, one of the group leaders. Ali was not only in charge of the project team but also responsible for research materials.

'How far it is from the station?' Ali inquired.

'About a twenty-day walk, if there is no problem on the way. Sometimes if it rains heavily, we have to stop. We cannot cross the river when the current is too strong,' Mohamad explained.

'That means more than a month for the collection?' Ali confirmed.

'Yeah! Or it could be more than that, because we have never been there. A lot of things we don't know may pose problems before we get there,' Mohamad explained further. He was an experienced research assistant who had spent all his life on research expeditions organised on the island. He came from the local area.

'If that is the case,' Ali declared, 'we must start our expedition, and the sooner the better.'

'Let us rest for a few days. Then we can start the expedition to the area,' Mohamad suggested.

'All right! Inform the others to be ready by Saturday. We will begin the journey to the area then,' Ali said, closing the discussion.

At my quarters, I was busy doing the indexes for the research project. There was a lot of documentation that had to be done as the project went on. These documents included coding procedures, indexes for the sorting out of the ingredients, mode of quality control, and so forth. Fortunately, a well-equipped facility for research work had been installed. The recording and indexing was easy to do.

I was still not able to sleep, so I started up my computer to check my email. I was surprised to see my email box full of documents regarding the island and its natural treasures. They had been sent by various organisations that I had been in contact with before coming to the station. One document was about an expedition made by a well-known explorer to the island in the fifth century.

There had been several groups of researchers working on the island. Most of them were researching the animals and endangered species. A lot of their work was published in international journals.

I was so engrossed in reading the reports, I didn't notice the time passing. My wife had prepared coffee and cakes for me, and I had not noticed her coming to the room. After reading almost all the documents, I felt physically and mentally tired. Without much ado, I fell asleep.

Suddenly, I was in the middle of a thick jungle, searching for seeds. I found them among the other fruit trees. I took most of the seeds and some edible fruits. After I had eaten some of the fruits, as I was to leave the place, I saw a tiger. The animal looked fierce and ready to make a move. As I turned to run, the animal made a quick movement of its paws and started running towards me.

I ran as fast as I could to save myself. However, the animal was so much faster that in no time, it was almost within an arm's length of me!

That's when I woke up. It was only a bad dream. My wife was sound asleep beside me. It was three in the morning, too early to get up, so I went back to sleep again.

CHAPTER 5

There was a lot of noise outside our quarters. It was still pitch dark, and the lights in the station compound were misty. There had been a heavy rain, and the compound was partly inundated by water. This was a normal tropical phenomena – heavy rain every now and then.

The expedition group was busy sorting out the equipment for the trip. The group consisted of fifteen people, including my wife and me. We had been selected from the five main groups and assigned specific tasks. Some would be seed collectors, some would be sorting out the seeds, and others would be coding and indexing the seeds collected.

Early that morning, we began the journey to our unknown destination. What we knew about the area came from stories narrated by the natives and the documents of past explorers. It was said that deep in the jungle, there was a huge area where certain plants that produce the medicinal ingredients we were after could be found. It was reported that even taken raw, the seeds could provide energy and cure gout, thyroid problems, and chronic diseases like malaria. They were also effective for relief of arthritis pain.

The place was said to never have been visited or explored. The locals could only relate what had happened to those who came upon the place by accident.

There was a story of a captain who came to the island to get some water for his ship. While on the island, after the crew collected some water, they saw a storm approaching. The crew and captain rushed to their boat on the beach. When the storm was raging with the rain, the captain lost his way. The crew could not find the captain and finally went to the ship without him. It was said that the captain was found by the natives and led to the area. He lived more than a hundred years with the help of the seeds found on the island.

This was just a story. It needed to be confirmed by study and research.

'Are you all ready to go now?' asked Ali in front of the group that had just been briefed on the expedition.

'We are ready!' we answered.

'All right. We will go in two groups. One group will take the route on the left, the other the route on the right,' Ali instructed the group members. My wife and I went with the group using the route on the right. Ali led the other group.

The jungle track was filled with a variety of plants. The route had long been used by the natives to track animals, such as reindeers and wild boars. Bones and skeletons of animals littered the way – the remains of what they had gathered and cooked. It was easy for the group to follow the track.

After a few days, our group came to a river. It was quite wide and too deep to cross on foot. We had to make a raft from bamboo and tree trunks. The current was strong, and it was only after several attempts that we reached the other side. Fortunately, all the equipment for the expedition was still in good condition.

'Let's camp here for a while before we continue our journey,' Lamin suggested. He had been given the duty of leading our group.

'Are we going to stop here for long?' asked one of the group members.

'If everybody gets some good rest and is ready to continue, we will move on immediately,' Lamin replied.

We all rested in a temporary tent that had just been erected. Some laid on the hard ground; some indulged in food and drinks. Before we could resume our journey, it began to rain again. At first it was drizzling, but a few hours later, it began to rain heavily. The tent could hardly withstand the heavy downpour.

The area slowly flooded with water. We had to move to higher ground further upriver. We settled down at the river confluence, which had a good view of the upper part of the river with its flowing current.

The rain continued to pour. It seemed as though it was going to rain for a long time. Lamin decided to make a more permanent camp so that we could rest comfortably.

'We have to stay here for the night. The rain may not stop for quite a while,' Lamin informed us all. The group erected two tents, one for my wife and me, the other for the rest of the group. By the time the work was finished, it was already dark. Some of the members were preparing food for dinner. That night, with the rain continuously pouring, the group members went to sleep early.

I was able to tune in a local radio station which was high-powered and equipped with the latest technology. I heard reports that the island had been buffeted by heavy storms since we had left the station. The storms had caused a lot of destruction in the villages along the beach. However, the storm had not spread widely inland yet. This phenomenon sometimes happened on the island: some parts experienced heavy rain and thunderstorms while others were unaffected.

It continued to pour the next morning. The group decided to stay in place. At midday, without any warning, the river began rising rapidly, finally reaching the campsite. The water current from upriver was strong and started overflowing onto the riverbank. Seeing the impending danger, Lamin instructed the members to make small huts at the tree trunks to avoid being swept away by the river.

We were all at the tree-trunk huts when the water from the river crashed into our campsite. It was like a tidal wave from the upper side of the river.

'Hold tightly to the tree trunks!' shouted Lamin as another wave of water approached the huts.

'All right. We are holding on tight!' the others cried out.

With full force, the water overwhelmed the whole area. Once the huge volume of water passed, the river returned to normal.

'Now we are safe. We can rest for the night,' Lamin assured us. The water was flowing at normal speed.

Fortunately, the tree trunks had been able to withstand the onslaught. We were all stunned and a bit panicky but unhurt.

The next day, all the water had receded, and we could see the debris scattered all over the place. That night, we were still at the tree-trunk camp. Early the next morning, the group decided to move on.

'Is everybody ready to continue our journey?' Lamin asked the group when we assembled for a short briefing.

'Yes! Let's move on,' we replied.

'This time, we'll have to follow the river. We are not sure whether certain areas in the jungle are flooded or not. It would be better to be near the river,' Lamin explained. This was because the area right along the river was normally higher than the surrounding area because of river silt and soil accumulating at the river banks.

We began our journey at Nanga Mujong by following the riverbank. It was said that the river's source was in a mountain not far from where the seeds were found. Fifteen days later, the group had reached the uppermost part of the jungle. Some members were truly exhausted and weary. Luckily, none of us got sick.

We stopped at an area in which the jungle was densely occupied by huge trees of various types. Trees that the locals called meranti, kapur, selangan batu, and belian (teak wood) were among them. Some of the trunks were so huge, it took a couple of minutes to get to the other side. They were so high you could hardly see the tops. There were a lot of animals running around, such as reindeer, wild boar, mouse deer, and monkeys hanging from the trees. However, there was no sign of tigers, leopards, elephants, or rhinos.

Various type of plants could be on the ground. Some had not been seen before by any of the group members. It was really fascinating to see these plants bearing flowers and leaves of many shapes and colours. Perhaps we had come to our destination – we weren't sure. It seemed that the area was of special significance, with all the little animals like rabbits, wildcats, and monkeys dashing around as if they were going about their normal life. They were not the least bit scared by our presence.

'This area seems to be a good place for our camp,' Lamin informed everybody.

'All right. Let's start putting up the tents,' one of the group members suggested.

'Before that, let me remind everybody that no one is allowed to wander about without permission,' Lamin said.

'How about if we want to venture a bit?' asked a member who had recently joined the research team.

'Not in this area of the jungle. We have to keep a close watch on each other. We never know what danger lurks here!' Lamin explained. He had a vast amount of experience in security matters after following several expeditions.

After putting up the tents, the team began its cooking for the day. It was late afternoon, and the weather was fine. Lamin and a few others were preparing for the next day, when they planned to go to an area further along to search for the seeds.

That night, everybody got some good rest in preparation for the following day. I was unable to sleep the whole night. I had a stomach ache and had to go to the loo several times. Just before I returned to my tent, I happened to see some lights in the distance. I quickly informed Lamin about it, and a few of us went to investigate.

After walking quite a distance, we were unable to locate the lights. They seemed to be moving further and further away. Now we were not sure where we were. Lamin, who had experienced such a thing before, informed us to stay put. We remained there until daylight and then found our way back to camp.

Everybody was pleased to see us return and wanted to know what was going on, especially my wife. I narrated to them what had happened, and everybody felt relieved. This phenomenon sometimes happened in the jungle. I was told by my grandfather when I was young that it was just like a Fata Morgana in the desert. When we went nearer to it, it disappeared.

The next day, the group was divided into two. One half was given the task of finding the seeds of the plants and the other had to search closer to the campsite for a new species of seeds which had medicinal value. It had been reported in the document of a Chinese explorer that *Atractylodes chinensis* seeds were plentiful on the island. These seeds possessed effective components for traditional medicines that had been used for centuries in mainland China.

My wife and I went with the first group. We were expected to go as far as possible from the campsite and return only when we had found the seeds. The other group had to scout around the campsite only, as the area was occupied by many of the plants we were looking for.

Lamin led our group. There were seven of us, including my wife. We set out that morning towards the deeper part of the jungle. After walking for almost three quarters of the day, we came to an area that was like a wide field with no trees around. The area was wide open, and you could see for miles. We were amazed by the surroundings, and that in the thick of the jungle, there was such an open space filled with rare plants.

'Let us stop here. This could be the place we are searching for!' Lamin said.

We were amazed by the size and the phenomenal view of the area. It seemed that this was an exclusive part of the dense jungle and must contain valuable treasure.

CHAPTER 6

'Wow! What a place!' we exclaimed when we finally regained our senses. The area was a huge field full of various types of plants.

'This place is like one of the Wonders of the World,' said Hassan Kadir, one of our group members.

'Look at the flowers of various plants, with their colours. The plants are also of a different variety,' added Karim Latif, another member of the group.

'We are really lucky to be here. Even if we don't get the seeds, it's enough just to see this,' Hassan Kadir exclaimed.

'We need to get the seeds within the time available. That is our main objective,' I told everybody.

'All right. Let's get cracking now. Each and every one of you needs to collect as many seeds as possible before we return to camp,' Lamin reminded everybody as he passed a list of the plants that we needed to search for.

'Where will we meet after the collection?' one of the group members asked.

'We come back to this spot here,' Lamin said as he planted a tall stick with a piece of red cloth to indicate the place. The tall stick could be seen from far away.

The seeds were known by the locals as *umur panjang*, which meant 'long life'. Those who knew the seeds described them as similar to pumpkin seeds. They grew on the branches of the plants, which came in different sizes and shapes. The seeds' cover, which looked like a walnut shell, was quite tough to crack. It was the contents that was being extracted for medicinal purposes.

The seeds were being sought for making supplements. Most countries in the region produced their own herbal supplements, which were then exported worldwide. The business was so lucrative that competition among suppliers was always stiff.

Herbal and natural products had gained popularity due to their effective ingredients. More and more people worldwide were looking for a source of high-quality products. Some products were processed from natural sources to cure ailments or diseases, and some of these were derived from seeds, fruits, leaves, flowers, herbs, and plants, such as *Serenoa serrulata* and *Serenoa repens* (fruit), *Avena sativa* (seed), *Apium graveolens* (seed), *Tumera diffuse* (leaf), *Achillea millefolium* (flower), *Hypericum perforatum* (flower), *Scutellaria lateriflora* (herb), *Astragalus membranaceus* (whole plant), and *Capsicum frutescens* (fruit).

The search for a remedy to prolong life had persisted for centuries. Scientists more than ever were trying to find out how the human body aged. The field of longevity research was pursued the world over. Through such research, it was found that human cells constantly undergo division to maintain our physical being.

As human beings age, this process of cell division slows down and in some cases eventually stops. The phenomenon has been known to scientists for years; they call it *cellular senescence*. This critical element was behind just about everything associated with the aging process, both visible – such as the decline in healthy skin tissue – and hidden – such as tissue degeneration, mental decline, and organ failure.

Current research suggested that telomere shortening could be responsible for cellular senescence. When a cell divides, the telomeres shorten, and it appeared that a telomere enzyme could offset this phenomenon by keeping the telomeres long even as cells divide and replicate.

At that time, no drug or natural product had been developed to amplify telomere activity. This new discovery correlated with the element of free radicals, which had been reported on in scientific journals for years. Besides antioxidants, it seemed that other dietary elements showed promise for telomere-supportive activity. Among these were commonly recognized cell-nourishing vitamins and minerals along with RNA/DNA components, micronutrients, and botanical phytonutrients. The latter ingredients were what the research-project team at the station was currently studying.

All of us started our 'search and collect' task as instructed, spreading out to do our work. We were reminded to keep an eye out for the tall stick to make sure we were not lost. The day passed, and now it was almost dark. Everyone was at the rendezvous except a new member of the research project.

'What are we going to do?' asked one of the group members.

'What do you think, Doc? What should we do?' Lamin looked to me for an answer.

'We can't just leave him. We have to find him. Do something!' I told everybody.

'Let Lamin go looking with two more persons, and the rest of us will wait here,' one of the group members suggested.

'That's right, you all stay here, and Lamin, Jonid, and I will go and find him,' I said, nodding to Lamin and the one who had made the suggestion.

We went deeper into the jungle, searching for our lost colleague. Not too long after, we found him, and the four of us returned together. The fellow had been quite sick when we located him in the bush. He had vomited a few times. He had eaten some wild fruits which he thought were safe. He was still weak when we came to the spot where the rest of the group were waiting.

After giving him some medicine, we went back to the camp, keeping closely to the track we had used earlier. When we arrived at the camp, it was almost dawn. Those at the camp were a bit worried that something bad might have happened to us in the jungle.

The campsite was lit up with a few wooden huts built on stilts. Those who remained had cleared the area and erected a few huts. My wife and I were given a hut for ourselves. The rest of the members were divided according to their specific tasks in the other few huts.

The seeds we collected were placed in a bigger hut next to mine so that it would be easier for me to start with the initial work of sorting out the seeds and classifying them. The seeds collected were many, and it would take several days to arrange and do the coding.

Most of the seeds collected were the *umur panjang*; however, there were some others which we wanted to study further. That's why we needed to do the sorting.

'We will have to deal with the seeds collected for a while,' Lamin told everybody.

'Does that mean we have to stay in the camp?' asked the new member of the research project, now fully recovered from his ordeal.

'Yeah, each and every one of you has to do as instructed. If everything is done according to plan, we should be able to complete the task of classification and coding within weeks,' Lamin explained. The seeds were quite small in size, and each of us had filled a huge backpack. Thus, there was a large volume to deal with.

'Make sure you do your work by following the instructions given. This is to ensure that our work is done according to the research SOP,' I added.

For a whole week, the group members worked in earnest. Fortunately, we had no problem with food. Apart from our own rations, we were able to get a supply of meat in the area itself. Our general workers could easily hunt the wild game found in the area, so we did not need to go anywhere. We even had access to vegetables from the local plants. The area was self-contained with local greenery and fruits.

During our second week there, the other group arrived at the camp, and we were happy to be reunited. They had been a bit delayed because the route they took was full of thick forest. They had not found the seeds.

They erected a few more huts for themselves, and then the whole collection group was at the camp and helping with whatever needed to be done. We were like a big family. During break time, we would entertain each other, especially at night. Some would sing while the rest followed with a chorus. Another group played instruments and some even danced. Life at the campsite became lively and enjoyable.

One night when we were still at the campsite, a terrible thing happened. All but one or two of us were already asleep when suddenly, there was a loud noise like a bomb. It was the sound of thunder followed by lighting. It struck a huge tree about twenty-two kilometres from our camp. We remembered the tree, as we had stopped for a rest at the tree trunk on our way back to the camp.

The tree was suddenly on fire, and the flames spread quickly towards the area where the seed plants were located. The whole area became engulfed in flames. In the tropical rainforest, even after the trees were soaked with rainwater, once the flame was started – usually by a tall tree – the smaller trees would soon be engulfed by the fire.

As we watched the flames spreading over the place, we could hear the cracking sounds of trees being burned, smell the burning wood and leaves, even smell the animals who could not escape the burning fire. The fire spread quickly over the area, as the wind was blowing strongly.

It was a pitiful scene, seeing the animals running for their lives. All the plant species were burned to the ground. Most of the tall trees were charred. Fortunately, the fire did not spread to our campsite. It gutted everything in its path – including the whole area of seed plants, leaving an empty piece of land with nothing but bare black soil.

What a pity that the endangered plant species were destroyed by this natural disaster. Gone were the seeds which were sought after by researchers and nature lovers. The fire only subsided at dawn, and we could see for miles the empty area with nothing but ashes and charcoal.

We couldn't do much except confine ourselves to the camp during the disaster. It was the few of us who were not yet asleep who began sounding the alarm when the fire started burning the trees. We were relieved that none of us was harmed.

After the disaster, everybody seemed to be quiet most of the time and focused on work. We had to finish the work before we could go back to the main research station. The seeds had to be sorted so that we could process them the moment we reached the station. Moreover, it would be easier to transport the sorted-out seeds, as they would be separated from the branches.

'How much more work do we have to do?' asked Ali. He was quite anxious to go back to the main station. We had been away for more than two months. Everybody was anxious to know what was going on there.

'Just a couple more days,' Lamin said, after he got confirmation from me.

'Well, if that's the case, we should concentrate more on our work so that we can finish sooner,' Ali reminded everybody.

Every one of us took his words seriously and tried to expedite the work. When we were finally finished, we quickly packed our things and all our equipment and left for the main station. Lamin was appointed by the group to lead the way. The route we took was the one following the river which we had used on our way in.

When we arrived at the place where the flood had occurred, we found a lot of leeches and scorpions on the ground. There was still a lot of water as well. We could hardly walk past the area.

'What should we do? These creatures are hungry as hell. We won't be able to withstand them. They will suck our blood,' one of the members complained.

'Well, there is no other way but to pass through,' Ali told everybody. He couldn't think of an alternative.

'We may have one option,' I suggested. 'Why not start using rafts like we did before?'

'But it is still a long way downriver to where we made the crossing,' said Lamin.

'We still can use the rafts to go downriver,' said another team member.

'Correct!' agreed most of the members. They were so scared of the leeches and scorpions that they were willing to use any other available option.

'All right. If that is the case, we start making the rafts now,' said Lamin.

It took us just an hour to make the rafts using bamboo and tree trunks, which were plentiful in the area. We rowed downriver following the current. There was no untoward incident, and we safely reached the spot where we had crossed previously.

From there, we continued our journey back to the main station. It was almost dark on the evening we arrived at our destination. Those at the station were thrilled to welcome us back. It seemed that something had happened at the station, and the members eagerly awaited our return.

While we had been gone, there had been some problems with the administration. This happened possibly because both the team leader and I were not around. We were partly to blame for not being proactive in preparing the middle leaders to take over. Of course, we didn't anticipate that something unexpected would happen.

CHAPTER 7

It was about a week after we had returned from our expedition that we finally heard the full story of what had happened at the station. Not everybody was willing to talk about it – only a few. The others were scared of the new administration.

We were a bit surprised that such a thing could happen here.

Upon our return, Ali was told he was no longer the person in charge of day-to-day administrative duties. He was informed by the new administration that his place had been taken by an officer from the foundation HQ.

'The station is a mess,' said Mr Lim Hong Fatt, a biochemist. He had been part of the research project team since the beginning.

'How did this happen? What is the story?' Ali asked.

'When you were not around, the administration was in a shambles,' Mr Lim tried to explain.

'That shouldn't be. All the staff were supposed to behave as professionals,' I said, joining the conversation.

'The seniors never agreed with each other. There were heated arguments almost every day,' Mr Lim explained further. During our expedition, a few seniors had been given the task of keeping up the daily routine at the station.

Unfortunately, it turned out that they had not been on good terms with each other before that.

'What happened then?' Lamin asked, as he joined in also.

'A few weeks after you people left, there was a heavy storm in the area,' Mr Lim said.

'It could be the same as the one at our campsite,' I said.

'The station was ravaged by the storm. We had no electricity, and we were in total darkness for weeks,' said Budin Long, an agro-scientist. He was one of those given the task of running the station.

'How about the spare generator? Wasn't it to be used in such situations?' Ali asked.

'That should have been the case. But nobody was willing to make the decision. The seniors never agreed on whether to use it or not,' Budin explained.

'That is the problem when authority is given to so many people,' I said.

'What happen then?' Lamin asked.

'Because of the problem, HQ sent Mr Malcom Green from the foundation's branch in Jakarta to take over the administration of the station,' Mr Lim said.

'With Mr Green in charge, everything was restricted. Everyone had to follow the new procedure,' Budin explained.

'Who made the new rules?' Ali asked.

'Mr Green, of course!' Budin said.

The staff at the research station had been quite friendly with each other. But with the introduction of the new regulations, they were now quite suspicious. The new administrator focused on work and discipline. He would not tolerate sloppiness or even a hint of complacency. Action had been taken against those who tried to flout the rules he enforced.

Since the mechanical problem, nobody was allowed to enter the generator area without his permission. It so happened that other equipment was stored in the same area. Whoever needed to go and fetch any equipment had to get permission first. Gone were the days when the staff was easy-going. Those who were not used to so many restrictions tended to protest, although it had to be done silently.

One day, something happened with the power generator, and there was a blackout. The whole staff was required to assemble in the courtyard the next morning. They were being admonished and asked to name the person responsible. In fact, the problem was mechanical, not the work of sabotage. Nobody should have been blamed for it. This was just an unprofessional act, as if the station was a factory or a school.

Nobody was willing to disclose anything. Everybody was unhappy with the situation. However, Mr Green would not compromise and insisted that an investigation must be carried out immediately. The investigation was done, and a few staff were given an ultimatum to resign or be sacked. The accused were upset because they had not done anything to the generator. They were only in the area to get some sport equipment, and in fact, permission had been granted for them to be there. But their plea was ignored. Five of them were sacked, including two professional staff.

One of the professionals was my close friend Andrew Philip. He was from New York and a good social scientist who cared for the welfare of the foundation staff. In fact, he had been recruited to ensure that the staff were well looked-after, as the station was far from other settlements.

Following that incident, the atmosphere in the station was tense and unpredictable. This was not conducive at all to a thriving research project. However, those who remained could not do much except proceed with the work as usual.

It was said that Mr Green had formerly worked with the Global Intelligence Agency. He had been posted in several countries to serve as an intelligence networking agent. Most of those who worked with him had found it difficult to forge a good relationship. This was partly because of his work background and training. However, due to his knowledge and exposure in the region, the foundation had recruited him to be one of its top officials on security.

He had been sent to the research station as a trouble-shooter to ensure that the research project was being carried out successfully. Much to the dismay of the staff and workers, Mr Green continued with his iron-clad style of administration.

One day, a few of us were called to his office. He wanted us to brief him on the progress of the research project. Being the chief person in charge of the programme, I was asked to make a presentation on the latest developments.

I presented a brief report and left time for questions. This was a normal research report presentation. By questioning, I assumed he could go deeper into the subject and understand more. However, my assumption was wrong. He was used to being given a briefing with detailed information. He was not happy and informed us that he would send a report to HQ that the research team members were not doing their jobs.

'Mr Green, if you intend to send a report to HQ, we have to be informed about the content of the report,' I said, as any professional would.

'No! No way. That is my prerogative,' he retorted. He seemed to be angry.

'We are professional people. You cannot simply do what you think,' I told him politely.

'Why not? I was sent here to see that the work is done,' he argued. But he was a bit diplomatic by then and lowered his voice.

'That is true. But at the same time, you must take into account what the people have done,' I again politely explained. He kept quiet for a while. He was trying to make sense of my explanation.

'Mr Green, this research work is not like other work. It takes longer to produce results,' Ali tried to explain.

Mr Green remained silent. He might have realised that he had been too harsh with us.

'More often than not, the outcome from a research project is not immediate. It has to be tested again and again,' Mr Lim joined in to explain what normally happened in research work.

After a long pause as he tried to make sense of what we had told him, Mr Green finally agreed with us.

'All right – in that case, I want you people to prepare the report on the progress of the research, and I will send it to HQ with my comments,' he said.

'Agreed,' all of us said with relief.

After that briefing and extended discussion, Mr Green seemed to understand better the real situation on the ground. He was quite accommodating towards our views on what actually happened at the station.

However, we were yet to see whether he would really change and become more open towards the staff's well-being.

It might not be that easy for somebody who had been given such authority to be more accommodating, especially when it touched on his area of expertise. Thus, Mr Green was still very strict with the rest of the staff and always wanted them to follow the rules. The staff gave him what he wanted. They didn't want to see the project fail and everybody lose.

CHAPTER 8

The staff and workers were now processing the seeds into ingredients that would be tested for medicinal benefits. The scientists and analysts needed to get the extracts and experiment on them. The extraction process had to be done systematically to ensure complete extraction of active herbal constituents. The result was then tested and retested to assure standardized potency of active ingredients.

'How far are you with the processing of the seeds now?' asked Mr Green. We were called again to present the latest progress of the processing work. He seemed to be anxious as time passed by.

'It seems that we are more or less done,' I said politely.

'Now we were in the process of standardizing potency and quality,' Mr Lim added.

'All right. That's good. How long do you think it will take until you have the end product?' Mr Green asked.

'Possibly within three weeks if everything goes well,' I confirmed.

'Okay, let's hope everything runs smoothly then,' Mr Green said, closing the discussion.

The research group had worked very hard to ensure that the result would not only be valid but also, more importantly, give the highest benefits. We had been processing the seeds with care and precision.

A few of us were called by Mr Green to his office to be informed that a group of important people were coming to the station to verify our work. These people were from Japan and included some businessmen. At first, we were reluctant to do what Mr Green wanted because this was a private arrangement between him and the group. The foundation had not been informed. He assured us that the meeting was just a discussion of the research.

We agreed on the condition that he informed the foundation. He agreed to do so, but he also cautioned us not to tell the others. The meeting was to be attended by the five of us only.

Before the group was due to arrive, I was given leave to go back home with my wife. We were to see our family after being at the station for more than five years. I brought with me most of the important documents regarding the seeds which had been processed, including the specimens and the formula to manufacture them into supplements. I left these with an agency back home before I went back to the station. I returned alone, as my wife wanted to attend to our grandchildren. The documents available at the station now were mostly from our initial work. I did that because I had a hunch Mr Green was up to something and not telling the truth about the meeting with the Japanese group.

When the group came, we were called by Mr Green for a closed-door meeting. Mr Green required us to brief the group about the end product of the research and how it could be turned into a supplement.

I gave the briefing, but most of what I told them was basic information. The other three members of the research group – Mr Lim, Ali, and Lamin – were a bit surprised. But they kept quiet. I needed to do what could be considered an offence under a confidentiality clause for research work in order to safeguard the foundation's interest.

After the briefing, Mr Green called his personal guards – whom he had appointed before the arrival of the Japanese group – to escort us to his main office, leaving the Japanese in the laboratory with him. We were not surprised by his actions and had expected something fishy. Mr Green had seemed strange in his behaviour.

'Why did you not tell the Japanese group the actual progress of the research?' Mr Lim asked when we were no longer with the visiting group.

'I have a hunch that something is not right about Mr Green's actions,' I told the three. But they still put their trust in Mr Green, as he had been appointed by the foundation. We had some confidence that he wouldn't do something detrimental to the foundation's interest.

'What is he intending to do?' asked Ali.

'I am not sure. But the way he met the group seemed to show that he had some kind of an arrangement that might jeopardise the outcome of the research,' I said.

'What should we do?' Lamin asked when we arrived at the main office.

'See, we are being escorted here, and the personal guards are always guarding us. Anyway, let me message HQ about what is going on,' I said.

'You still have your Blackberry?' asked Mr Lim.

'Yes, I hid it in my briefcase,' I told them.

I was able to send the messages – including an SOS – before Mr Green gave instructions to confiscate all our belongings. We were confined to the main office with locked gates guarded by security men. We were not allowed to go out or communicate with the others.

Meanwhile, Mr Green was with this group trying to ascertain whether the results of the research could be used. Scientists from Japan had been brought in to assist them. Their effort was futile; the scientists did not have the experience to do the job.

At last, they came back to us to request that we disclose the outcome. But we refused to co-operate because of the way Mr Green had treated us. When they could not convince us to help, they kept us locked in the room at the main office. We were still waiting for HQ to respond to our request.

Through a small window in the room, we could see more and more Japanese personnel entering the research station. They needed time to secure the outcome of the seed processing. Without our help, it would be hard to get results. They anticipated that the foundation would find out what was going on and were preparing to defend the station in case of attack. The station was like a fortress closely guarded by Japanese yakuza gang members.

There was a lot of movement of heavy machinery and guns into the area. Japanese personnel were all over the place. The station was like a war zone bustling with army activity, as if they were gearing for a battle.

The station was no longer doing its main activity. The Japanese were taking over the whole area. The staff were being kept in their places of work. Much to the dismay of everybody, there was no longer any communication between the groups. It seemed that the station was being prepared for something unprecedented to happen.

CHAPTER 9

We were kept as captives for almost a week, with no access to information and no idea what was going on outside the main office building. We were kept in a room guarded by yakuza. They were known for their brutality when dealing with opponents. The members were signed as blood brothers. They were willing to do anything their boss asked of them.

Fortunately, the office was stocked with our daily needs – food, drinks, beds, clothing, and so on. But we were not allowed to go outside our room.

We were not sure whether the foundation had sent a rescue team. There was no way to know what was going on. The gang members spoke in their own language and paid no attention when we called out to them.

'What should we do, Doc?' Ali asked me. We began discussing our situation.

'What do you think, Mr Lim?' I asked. Mr Lim seemed to be unworried about the whole situation; he was always looking at things in a positive manner. That's why he seldom faced any problems when working.

'We may have to wait for some time. The foundation people will soon know what is going on at the station,' he said in a matter-of-fact way. He was calm and able to smile when he said those words.

'We can't just wait! We have to do something!' Ali said.

'Why not try to get out of this building?' Lamin finally suggested.

'How? We are kept in locked-up room,' Ali said.

'If there is a will, there is a way,' Lamin said, remembering my earlier words of advice.

'All right. Let's discuss it,' I agreed.

After a long discussion, we decided to escape through the ceiling of the room and go out to the roof. We waited until nightfall and then made a move. Mr Lim, even though at first quite reluctant to consider the idea, finally went along with us. Lamin, who knew the structure of the building, led the way.

'Follow me,' Lamin said as we crawled across the rooftop.

'Look, there are guards all over the place,' Mr Lim said. We continued crawling as the guards went about their business.

'Not too loud,' Lamin reminded us.

When we reached a tall tree next to the building, Lamin again cautioned us not to talk loudly.

'Are we to jump down from the tree?' Ali asked.

'No! We go down using a tree branch. Go slowly and quietly!' Lamin whispered.

We were finally able to escape the building using a tree branch located quite close to the building and got out of the station compound by cutting the wire fence. Lamin was able to get the equipment we needed. Once out of the compound, we headed straight for the nearest jungle. From there, we walked all the way to the border of Malaysia and Indonesia. Lamin, being a local, knew the route quite well. We reached our destination the following day, after travelling about 150 kilometres.

At the border, we met some workers from the research station. They told us that there was a gun battle after we left. They described what they saw when they made their escape. The two groups were fighting each other using the latest firepower. Mr Green and the Japanese gang were surrounded by the attacking group, but the workers weren't sure who that was.

We felt relieved to have been able to escape from the station. From the Indonesian side of the border, I was able to contact a former colleague, Muliyadi Jokowi. We had studied together at the same university in the United Kingdom before I did my study in Australia. I was able to contact him for assistance in getting off the island. My friend, with the help of the local people, brought us to the main town. From there, we took a plane to Jakarta.

We stayed for a few days in Jakarta, undecided on what to do next.

'What do you think we should do now, Doc?' Ali asked me.

'I am not so sure. We cannot contact the foundation at the moment, because we don't know to which group Mr Green belongs,' I explained.

'We also don't know who will be coming to the station from the foundation side!' Mr Lim joined in.

'We lay low for a while until we know the actual situation at the research station,' I advised.

We all stayed at the same hotel, Hotel Grand Indonesia. I was able to get some money from the local bank, which allowed international transactions. We tried to get as much information as possible regarding what had happened at the research station.

The rescue team had actually been sent by foundation HQ upon receiving my message. They came to the island with a fleet of helicopters. Under the command of Captain James Steward, they surrounded the station. However, the Japanese gang resisted intensely. For several days, the gun battle raged until the Japanese gang was defeated. Mr Green was captured with his accomplices, including the Japanese yakuza leader. They were all brought to the United States and charged for their dangerous activity. This was done with the agreement of the Malaysian authorities. They were found guilty and imprisoned for life.

The foundation team didn't know that the four of us were alive because during the assault on the main office building, it was burned to the ground. We were presumed dead by the rescue team, and the foundation was informed about it. The laboratory, which was defended by the Japanese gang closely, was also burned to the ground. With that, all the research materials were lost, and there was no trace of the research work left.

After we learned about the situation at the research station, we decided not to reveal our identity to the foundation and kept hiding. We were still not sure about Mr Green's connections. It would be safer to lay low for the time being.

We decided to go our separate ways and do whatever we intended to do for ourselves. Ali and Lamin returned to Malaysia, and Mr Lim went to Singapore. At first, I wanted to go back to Malaysia and join my family. However, something happened while I was at the US embassy checking for updates regarding the foundation's latest news that changed my plans.

The assistant high commissioner of the embassy was suspicious of my enquiry. He had been Mr Green's colleague while they were serving together in the region. I got this information from the embassy staff. Soon after, I was detained for routine questioning. I was kept at the embassy for a few days and not allowed to go out.

One day, my friend, who was happening to apply for a visa, saw me when I was on the way to meet the embassy officer for further questioning. He asked the embassy staff if he could meet with me. He was given permission, possibly because the embassy did not want my detention to become an issue.

I asked my friend to help me with my release. With assistance from the Indonesian authorities, I was finally allowed to leave the embassy. I stayed a few more days in Jakarta before leaving Indonesia for good.

I contacted my wife and let her know that I intended to go to Amsterdam and wanted her to join me. I had been attracted by European cities when I studied in United Kingdom. Fortunately, I had brought my passport with me when we escaped from the research station. Three of us were able to get hold of our passports, which were kept in a cabinet in the main office, before we were held in the room. I decided to go to Amsterdam because, if I need to go to the foundation's HQ, it would easier for me to go from there. Moreover, I had very much wanted to travel there, as I'd heard a lot about the place.

The following day, my friend sent me to the Soekarno-Hatta International Airport, and I boarded a KLM flight to Holland. I stayed at Hotel 5 while I waited for my wife to arrive, but she had to go back home when one of our grandchildren became seriously ill.

I was by myself in the big city and yet to find acquaintances. During the day, I would go about the city centre and spend my time in bookshops. Sometimes I would go for a river cruise, which took me through various canals around the city's outskirts. This was how I mostly spent my time.

Amsterdam was a beautiful city and always peaceful. I could go about doing what I wanted without much problem. The people were friendly and helpful when I needed assistance. I felt like I was back home. Most of the time, I would go window-shopping and enjoy the city.

The city centre was crowded with tourists from all over the world. I could easily meet my countrymen while walking along the busy street. People from all walks of life were busy with their daily routines. The city was full of foreigners who came and went for their businesses. I was really fascinated by the easy-going atmosphere. You could go around without much thought of being scared. This feeling of peacefulness, which was a hallmark of the city, had existed since the city became the port of call for Europe.

The port was always busy with ships and cargo. It was a beautiful place, and tourists flocked to see the ships loading and unloading goods from all over the world.

CHAPTER 10

Walking alone in the city centre one day, I felt excited to be in a city I had longed to visit for so many years. The first place I went to, as always, was a bookshop. After spending some time looking at books, especially the new arrivals, I continued my walk.

When I saw a group of people lined up in front of a building, I thought there must be something interesting going on, so I joined the crowd. In fact, it was a wax museum, Madame Tussauds, which attracted many visitors. I visited as well to see the displays inside.

After that, I went to various stalls selling all kinds of souvenirs situated along the riverbank. From one stall to another, I followed the crowd of tourists looking for anything of interest. Then I went to a row of shops where a live show of women tried to entice passers-by to become their customers. It was while I was looking at the show that I was surrounded by a few men who forced me to follow them into a car.

They drove me to a harbour area and brought me to a warehouse, where they questioned me about what they thought I was involved in: an international prostitution syndicate with which their group had a business dealing. It seemed they had been observing my movements for quite some time. When they saw me at the shop, they took their chance to grab me.

'Are you from South Africa?' one of the fellows asked. He was tall with long hair, and I heard his friends call him Tattoo Bolt. His hands were mostly covered by tattoos.

'No, I am from Malaysia,' I said.

'But look at this photo. Is that not you?' The face of the man in the photograph did have features similar to mine.

'I have never been to South Africa. That man is not me!' I told him.

'Cannot be! You look like him. We are searching for him. He has taken away our business,' Tattoo Bolt said.

I looked carefully at the photograph. I was able to make out one difference between the person in the picture and me.

'No, that is not me. Look carefully at his forehead. There is a slightly visible scar, but I don't have one.'

He looked again at the photograph. Although he was still not convinced, he stopped questioning.

'All right. If that is the case, we will let you go free,' he said finally.

I was so relieved. They took me back to the city centre, and I quickly returned to my hotel. After that incident, I decided not to walk freely about the city centre anymore. I spent my time mostly in the hotel.

I was still very much interested in continuing to work with the foundation. The seed business was always on my mind. I tried to check through social media about the research station and the foundation's interest in the matter. I couldn't get much information. I hoped that by being in Amsterdam, I would be able to avail myself of the opportunity sometime soon.

I had been in Amsterdam for about a month when I decided to find a job and applied as a research officer at a local company. My work with the foundation was not mentioned, as I didn't want to be asked about it. The interview was successful, and I was hired.

My first posting was in Russia. The company was researching the extension of human life in urban areas. The first urban area to be researched was Moscow, because it had a large population of senior citizens among its urban population. They came from rural areas and were said to live much longer than the others. The research was to study the pattern of their lives that led to that longevity.

It was in Moscow that I once again met Andrew Philip, my former research fellow from the station in the jungles of Malaysia. He was employed by a private agency, Russian International Human Rights. Andrew was a reliable worker as well as trustworthy.

'What have you been doing since you left the station?' I asked.

'At first, I worked in New York with a local research marketing agency. It was good exposure for me in the field of marketing and overseas connections. That's how I came in contact with my current employer,' he explained.

'I am pleased to see you, Andrew,' I said. We had been quite close when he was working with the foundation at the research station.

'I am also happy to meet you and continue with our acquaintance,' he said before we parted.

Now I had somebody I could talk to and confide in about anything of importance. Because he left before the research station was raided, Andrew was unaware of what had happened. He thought I was still working with the foundation. I told him the whole story, and he was happy that I had been able to get away from the island.

From the information I could gather through social media – though there was not much – it appeared that mystery shrouded the research project in the later stages of the enterprise. The idea of extending human life was noble initially. But when some members of the board wanted the product to make a profit rather than benefit customers, the result was conspiracy and intrigue. Only a few of them stuck to the original plan. When trouble came, there seemed to be no longer much interest in the idea.

However, a few board members who were keen to continue with the research were willing to give it another try. It was through Andrew that I was able to communicate with them, and they were happy to know that I was still alive. I was invited to come to New York to discuss the matter. I asked Andrew whether he would like to come along. With him, I would not be lost in New York, since he came from the city. He agreed.

I took a few days leave and went to New York with Andrew to meet the board members. The five members who were still keen to continue with the research project met me at the foundation HQ in Manhattan. It was located on the fifty-sixth floor of one of the tallest buildings in the area.

'How are you, Mr Zaidi?' asked Hebert Kerry. He was the most senior among the board members.

'I am fine, sir,' I said.

'So you were able to get away before the station was raided?' he continued.

'Yes, a few of us were able to escape from captivity. We went to the border,' I explained.

We had a long discussion, and it seemed that they were still interested in conducting the research. They had confidence in the project we had started. Moreover, they believed from the information they had been given before the station was raided that the seeds had real potential to become a product for making health supplements of high quality. They were contemplating making a second attempt at the research that had stopped so abruptly.

They still had to search for a new place to carry out the project. I would be informed once they got that place. They would appoint me as research fellow, as they had done previously.

Andrew and I spent a few days in New York before heading back to Moscow. During our stay in the city, I was able to visit some famous landmarks, including the Empire State Building, World Trade Centre, United Nations, and renowned shopping areas. Andrew also took me to his hometown, located a few kilometres away in the outskirts of the city.

Once back in Moscow, I continued with my work. The research project was to include a few more cities for the purpose of comparison. The team conducted research in Paris, Rome, and Madrid. After a few months, the project was completed, and the company was to make known the outcome.

It was discovered that urban living required a lot of complementary infrastructure and added-value facilities for the older folks. Since most of these cities had such infrastructure and facilities, older citizens who had moved from rural to urban areas were able to benefit from them. They were, in fact, able to prolong their lives and enjoy urban living.

The project was a huge success, and the company was awarded a substantial sum of money by the various governments, which used the data and statistics for their development planning and programme implementation. I was paid handsomely and offered another research project. However, I turned it down. I was waiting for an offer from the foundation to continue with the project that was abandoned due to the incident on the island.

I was again without a job and spent most of my time reading and visiting places in Amsterdam and the surrounding area. After a while, I decided to go back to Malaysia to see my family. I booked a ticket and was scheduled to fly on Saturday. Before leaving Amsterdam, I thought I'd go around the city centre and buy something to take home.

While I was in the bookstore buying some books, I was surrounded by another group of men who wanted me to follow them. They seemed to be quite decent, with proper attire and a polite manner when they talked to me and introduced themselves.

'Sir, may we, if you don't mind, asking you to follow us to see our boss?' one of them said. I learned later that his name was John Clinton.

'May I know what this is about?' I asked.

'We are not sure. Our boss just informed us to bring you to see him,' he continued.

'Well, if it is something that is not detrimental, I guess I will accede to your request,' I replied.

'Good. We all assure you that nothing will happen to you,' he said.

Trusting that they meant well, I followed them. Truly, I did not have much of a choice. I was brought to a room in a hotel nearby which was quite close to the hotel I was staying at. In fact, I had wanted to stay at that hotel but changed my mind at the last minute. Possibly the boss was staying there in the belief that I would be as well. After all, the hotel was prominently located and well known.

The boss turned out to be one of the board members of the foundation. He had not joined much of the discussion in New York with the other members, although he did introduce himself to me. During that discussion, he was mostly jotting down notes on his iPad.

Now, he introduced himself again. 'I am Mr James Cunningham, one of the board members of the foundation,' he said.

'Well, Mr Cunningham, I am Mr Zaidi,' I replied.

'We already met at the foundation HQ, right?' he said.

'Yes, I remember meeting you there,' I told him.

Then he looked at me and said, a bit hesitantly, 'I would like you to tell me what have you done with the seed specimen'.

I was caught unprepared by the question. I looked at him, trying to figure out what he could possibly know about my actions to protect the research. 'The whole building burned to the ground. I assume the specimens were also burned. I was no longer there,' I said finally.

He looked me directly in the eyes. I was sitting across the desk from him. The fellows who had brought me there stood nearby.

'Is there a possibility that you removed the specimens before the incident occurred?' he asked.

'No. There is no possibility of that, as Mr Green kept an eye on what everybody was doing at the station,' I said confidently. I tried to be as natural as I possibly could and answer only what was being asked.

He did not seem convinced by my response. 'Did you go back to your hometown before the incident?' he questioned.

'Yes. I went back for a short leave, since I had not taken any for quite some time.'

'Did you bring back any documents and specimens?' he asked.

'No!' I answered without hesitation.

'Are you sure of this?' he demanded.

'Absolutely!' I answered back.

There was a long silence. He just looked at me, as if to ascertain whether I was telling the truth. I tried to act as normal as possible and continued to maintain eye contact.

After a while, he instructed his men to usher me out of the room. They brought me to another room and told me to wait there. If they didn't come back, I was free to leave the place. But as they closed the door, it locked itself from the outside. I was in the room alone, and now I felt a bit scared. I was not sure what was going on and why they had asked me to wait.

I waited for quite some time, but nothing happened. The room was a bit small, with barely any furniture except a table and chair. There was a ceiling fan which was a bit old and made some noise. It was the sort of spare room used for an extra guest when required.

I looked at my watch; it was almost five o'clock. I had been away from my hotel for almost the whole day.

Finally, I heard noises outside the room. The hotel workers were coming in for the night shift. I decided to get their attention by banging on the door. They fell silent at first, and then they knocked on the door. I shouted to tell them that the door was locked from the outside. They tried several keys to unlock it, and only after several attempts was the door finally opened. They were surprised to see me inside. I told them what had happened, and they brought me to see the management.

After a discussion with the management, I was allowed to go. I went quickly to my hotel and straight to my room. As I entered the room, suddenly I found myself caught by someone from the back, who blindfolded me with a piece of cloth. I was brought to a car, possibly at the back of the hotel. Since I had only eaten breakfast, I was very hungry and could no longer stand anymore. I just collapsed.

CHAPTER 11

When I woke up, I was on a bed in a huge room. A middle-aged lady came with a few men and asked whether I wanted dinner. I was still a bit dizzy but was able to think rationally. I looked at them and could sense that they were good people.

'I need to eat a proper meal. I'm very hungry,' I said in a begging tone.

'All right. We will provide you also with juice and coffee,' said the lady. 'Anything else you want, say a salad?' she asked.

'Some dessert, I guess!' I said.

'Just give us a few minutes, and we will bring in your food. Meanwhile, just relax and watch TV,' the lady said as she went out with the rest.

I wondered why I was being treated so well despite being brought in blindfolded. They came with all the food I had asked for. It was laid out on a huge table adjacent to my bed. The room was really nice and fully equipped with furniture.

'All right. Enjoy your dinner. After that, you can have a good rest. Our boss will come to see you in the morning,' the lady explained. Then they all went out, leaving me alone with the food on the table.

The room had a telephone and a PC with an Internet connection. Since I was being treated well, I assumed they meant well. I remembered what the earlier group had said to me; this could be the same group. I gave them the benefit of the doubt.

Still, I was not sure where I was – whether in a hotel or a private residence. As instructed, after I ate my food, I went straight to bed. I was really tired from my ordeal.

The next morning, I felt fresh and ready to meet the boss. While I was contemplating what had happened to me the previous day, the door opened. Mr Cunningham and a few others came in.

'Good morning, Mr Zaidi. How are you today?' he greeted me with a smile.

'I am fine!' I answered promptly.

'Well. Glad to see you again. I am very sorry for what happened to you yesterday,' he said in a regretful manner. I was a bit surprised to hear that.

'That's all right. I was not sure why I was being treated as if I had done something wrong,' I said. I asked for an explanation.

Mr Cunningham told me the whole story. He had been asked to meet me to discuss the foundation's new research project. However, when he came to Amsterdam, he was approached by an American businessman by the name of Van de Claff. This businessman had influenced him with a story that it was my fault the research project failed. He said that I had taken away the seed specimens. According to him, it was because of that Mr Green punished me and the other three by locking us in the main building.

Once he realised that the man was a professional trickster, even though there might be truth to the story, he immediately asked his acquaintances to rescue me from my hotel room. That was why I was caught from the back, blindfolded, and taken away secretly. They did it to show the businessman's people, who happened to be at the hotel, that they were taking some action against me.

'Now, do you know what happened to me after our meeting?' I asked Mr Cunningham.

'I thought they ushered you out and let you go,' he said.

'No, I was kept in a room which was locked,' I said.

'We didn't lock the room,' said one of the fellows who was standing by while I was talking with Mr Cunningham.

'Maybe it was self-locked and the lock was not working,' said another fellow who was standing next to him.

'That's possible. We are sorry for the unfortunate incident,' said Mr Cunningham. 'Now, let's discuss the research project as requested by the board members,' he said in a serious tone.

The research station had actually been rebuilt and was ready to be used, according to Mr Cunningham. People had been sent out to scout around in the area where the seeds had been found. It seemed that the area which was burned up in the fire was now already covered with plenty of new plants.

The foundation was in the process of recruiting professional staff and workers. In a few months, the project would be ready to get started. That was why the board had asked him to meet me for appointment to the research fellow job.

'Are you willing to accept the foundation's offer?' Mr Cunningham asked. He looked at me to see my reaction. There was a moment of silence. I was still not sure whether to accept the job. It was a big responsibility, especially now that the board members knew me personally.

'What happens if I don't accept the offer?' I asked, just to test the foundation's seriousness in the matter.

He looked at me directly and said, 'We really need you. You have done a great job previously, and now we know you personally,' he said.

'May I think it over first? I would like to see the station before I make my decision,' I finally said to him.

'All right. If that is what you prefer to do, I will inform the board members. We will wait for your decision,' he said finally.

'Thank you, Mr Cunningham,' I said, and we closed the discussion.

His men brought me to my hotel and stayed at the hotel to ensure my safety. That night, I contacted Ali, Lamin, and Mr Lim to inform them about the foundation's plan to continue with the research project. They received the news happily. I asked them to join me if I decided to become the research fellow again. They all gave a positive response.

That Saturday, I boarded a plane to go back home to Malaysia and re-join my family. After a few weeks, I was contacted by the foundation staff, who informed me that they were arranging my trip to the island via Singapore. I advised Ali and Lamin to be ready so that we could all go to Singapore for the trip to the island. We met Mr Lim and stayed a few days. My wife came with me this time. The next day, we proceeded to the research station in a helicopter.

We arrived at the research station and were warmly welcomed by the staff and workers. We were a bit surprised to see the modern set-up. There were security personnel, and the place was closely guarded. We were brought to the main office to meet the administration head. While there, we were treated like VIPs by the office staff. Soon we would be meeting the CEO of the station, who was in charge of its administration. When we were brought to his room, I was surprised to see that it was Mr Cunningham.

'Good morning, Mr Zaidi. How was your trip from Singapore?' he asked.

'Well, smooth going, Mr Cunningham. I am glad to see you again. Let me introduce to you to our former staff, who would like to join the team again.'

'Very good! So you have made your decision?' he asked, looking to see my reaction. There was a moment of silence. In fact, I had not made the decision yet, for I wanted to see the place first. But I had committed to the three that if they were willing to work for the foundation again, I would accept the offer.

'I guess I have to, Mr Cunningham. After all, my former colleagues agreed to work with the foundation.'

'That is good news for us. Let me show you around the main laboratory where you will be doing your research,' he said with a smile, inviting us to follow him.

The new station was well equipped with the latest technology and well planned. The complex took up most of the 150 hectares of the station area. Previously, the area was not fenced up, but now the entire station area had been fitted with security fencing. The number of buildings had also increased, along with the number of workers.

The foundation wanted the product of the research work to be of high quality and marketable. They did not mind spending a lot of money on equipment as long as they received a good return on the investment in the end. Mr Cunningham had been assigned to ensure that the professional staff and workers were well looked after. We were happy to assist him, as he was more people-friendly and professionally oriented than past administrators.

After the tour, Mr Cunningham left us to go to our respective quarters. My wife and I were given the one nearest to the laboratory. It was quite close quarters for the three who would be helping me take charge of the research programme.

We were to begin our work as soon as possible. Now that we had more than a hundred staff and workers at the station, we intended to continue with what we had done previously. I had taken with me the original documents and seed specimens from home. However, I kept them to myself and only used them when I needed them as reference.

For the first few months, we worked in earnest. We were able to gather some of the seeds that had been kept in stores that Mr Green was not aware of. They had escaped the blaze when the station was attacked. The analysis had been completed before the incident. Now we needed to test the potency of the ingredients by experimenting with people.

The control group for the experiment consisted of the staff and some workers, including my wife and myself. The experiment started with the consumption of the product and was to be monitored daily. After several months, the results would become apparent through analysis. The expected outcome was a product that could prolong human life.

CHAPTER 12

The participants in the control group undergoing the experiment were to report the outcome. This was to ensure that the effect of the test/trial product was really experienced by people. According to the analysis and the report from members of the control group, the product clearly had a significant effect.

'I felt more energetic than before after taking the stuff,' one member said.

'My overall health has totally improved in a dramatic way,' said another.

'The trial product does increase my energy,' reported a number of the members.

'The trial product makes me feel fit and full of energy,' said a lady member.

For my part, I really felt that my physical strength increased tremendously, and my mental power also showed a marked improvement. My wife and I were the oldest members of the group, and our report became the main focus of the research team. If the effect of the stuff was found to be sustainable, the product could be said to have high potency and good quality.

The report from the members of the control group was compiled. The trial product was found to have great potency in improving human health and wellness. Thus, it could help to prolong human life.

The next step was to verify further the trial product's quality and purity. This was done by following accepted international conventions. Quality credentials such as 'USP Verified' (for US products) or 'ConsumerLab.com Approved Quality' had to be obtained before the product could be processed for sale on the open market.

As the station was fully equipped with the latest facilities, the product could be processed on-site. The end product was formulated, mixed, placed in containers, and packed. The whole process underwent laboratory testing with routine quality control. All procedures met GMP and TGA standards and complied with the Food Act.

Now the research station was ready to market the product. Mr Cunningham appointed a few of us to visit various places to meet with prospective distributors. I was leading a group to Japan to promote the product. My wife, Mr Lim, and Lamin were joining me on the trip.

We met a few distributors when we were in Tokyo. After a promotional exercise, most of the distributors were keen to be our product agents. The news about us and the product spread all over the country after the media conference. We were in the news in most mainstream media for several days.

One day, we were enticed by a group of Japanese businessmen to come to a secluded place. They told us that they would gather more distributors for the product promotion. Forgetting what had happened at the research station previously, we went to the place without hesitation. At first, we were treated well by the host.

However, the following day, we were surrounded by angry businessmen who had failed to get the product from Mr Green and his associates. They thought that they had been cheated and demanded they be compensated for their investments.

'You have cheated us,' said Masaru Nishimori, the leader of the group.

'We were not involved with Mr Green's work. We were doing research for the product,' I told him.

'But at least you know, because you were there with Mr Green,' he insisted, certain that we had been involved in the business dealing.

'We were not involved in the business arrangement. Mr Green never informed us,' I said, trying to convince them.

'We want our money back, no matter what you tell us,' the others said.

They were not ready to negotiate. These businessmen really were interested in the product – there was great potential for the product in Japan. The Japanese were among those in the world who lived longer lives. They seemed to know a trick or two when it came to living beyond 100 years. According to a United Nations report, they had the greatest proportion of centenarians of any country around the globe.

'We will keep you in this place until your superior accedes to our request,' Masaru Nishimori said with a word of warning.

So we were held in the big mansion to await a response from the foundation HQ. While we were there, however, we were treated well by our host.

After a few days, the foundation HQ sent its officer to Japan to negotiate with the businessmen. The officer and the businessmen finally agreed that those who had invested in the venture previously were to be given their due share in the current product distribution and sale.

We were finally allowed to leave the mansion. The businessmen were happy and sorry about the ordeal we had undergone. We thanked them for the good treatment given to us and moved on to promote the product to other countries. We went to South Korea, Singapore, New Zealand, and Australia. The response from the distributors of health products in those countries was very encouraging. They signed the contract immediately, and we were pleased with the outcome of the trip so far.

Our next destination was Dubai. We were interested in distributing the product to the Gulf States, which we would also do through Dubai. The response given to our request for a meeting was positive. The Arabs were also keen to experience long lives.

However, when we arrived in Dubai, something unexpected happened. As soon as we landed and once we had entered the airport terminal, we were detained by immigration officials. We were brought to meet the Chief Officer, Al-Farouki Nazim.

'*Assalamualaikum (peace be upon you)*. How are you all?' he greeted us.

'*Mualaikumussalam (peace be upon you also)*. We are all well,' I responded.

'We have to detain you because of the goods you brought in,' he said, starting the interrogation.

'But there is nothing wrong with the goods. They are just supplement products for health,' I explained.

'We know that. We have to make sure that the product is halal,' he said. He told us that there was no certification for the product as halal (legal). Thus they needed time to check thoroughly, and we were to be detained for quite a while. There had been a tip-off that we were bringing in some illegal substance. The authorities had been given information that we were dealing with a syndicate in the region to distribute haram (prohibited) goods.

Some officials from the Malaysian embassy in the Emirates came to ask us about the product. We explained that we had been to a number of countries to promote it, and there had been no problem, even in countries belonging to the Association of Southeast Asian Nations (ASEAN), such as Indonesia, Brunei, and Singapore. We had not obtained halal certification for the product. Nevertheless, the product was accepted by the ASEAN countries as ingredients mainly from seeds of certain plants.

The problem was finally resolved after our embassy assured the immigration authority that the product was not haram. With that, we were able to promote the product not only in the Arab Emirates but in all the Gulf States. The product was well-received by the Arab population, and the distributors were happy to be involved in the business deals. We went on to promote the product in Egypt, Turkey, Saudi Arabia, and Iran. Our next target would be the European Union (EU) and the Russian Federation.

We started our promotional programme in Holland. I was quite familiar with the country, having stayed there for a while. At first, there was not much problem with the promotion. However, when an American businessman who was influenced by Mr Green came into the picture, we faced a lot of problems. This businessman by the name of Van de Claff – the same one who had caused me problems earlier by approaching Mr Cunningham – was able to influence some of the businessmen in Amsterdam to refuse to participate in our business deal.

In one of the meetings with local businessmen, Van de Claff made a fuss about our product. He stood up and started making remarks, trying to give a bad impression.

'How are we possibly to know that the product really gives us these benefits?' he asked in front of all those present.

'True. Can you give us proof that the products are really beneficial?' said one of his supporters.

'That's why we are having this meeting, so that we can explain to all of you about the product,' I explained.

'How are we to believe you?' Van de Claff asked.

'Well, apart from our record on the product in other countries, the proof of the pudding – whether it is good or not – is in the eating,' I said.

The other businessmen were in fact in favour of the product. They had the information already, and they were interested in the deal.

Early on, we were harassed and intimidated by local businessmen because of the misinformation being spread around by Van de Claff and his supporters. However, we persisted with our objective, and finally we were able to convince many of the businessmen to join our venture.

In the Russian Federation, I was able to get Andrew to gather businessmen to meet us. They were happy and willing to become our distributors for the product.

For the other countries, there were a few teams who went out to promote the product. They went to South

Africa, the United States, Canada, and South America. As a whole, the campaign to promote the product achieved it objective. Now the product was known around the globe.

However, before the product could be distributed to all these countries, there was yet another problem. This time, it was with production at the research station. The administration was not prepared for such an overwhelming response from distributors. There was a lot of competition from herbal-product suppliers in every country that had been on the market much longer and had a lot of customers. But although our product was quite new, it was more attractive to consumers because of its potency. Our research was so professionally done that the distributors could easily convince buyers of the quality of the product.

The research station had to find ways and means to increase production to meet the growing demand. Consumers had voiced concerns about not being able to obtain the product in large quantities. The foundation needed to find the quickest way of getting the seeds.

CHAPTER 13

The production section of the business was faced with a short supply of seeds for product processing. Mr Cunningham, who was happy with the promotional campaign, now found it difficult to resolve this problem. Demand from the distributors was overwhelming. Every distributor in each of the countries where there were business deals with the foundation wanted the product urgently due to great demand. The research station needed to resolve this problem.

'What do you think, Doc? Is there a way for us to get the seeds?' Mr Cunningham looked at me.

'I believe if there is a will, there must be a way,' I said philosophically.

'How?' Mr Lim asked innocently.

'Can we get the seeds from the place where we found them before?' Ali posed a question.

'That's one of the options we can consider. The other option would be to search for a new place in the same area,' I said.

'If we were to go there, how certain could we be about getting the seeds?' asked Mr Lim, beginning to consider the possibility.

'Since the incident took place quite a number of years back, I think the seeds would now be fully grown – provided the place was not visited by other people,' I told them.

'All right then, we send a team to check whether the seeds are available there,' Mr Cunningham said finally.

The following day, a team was dispatched to the place for an investigation. They went by helicopter, with Lamin as the leader. The team was supposed to check and let the station know if the seeds were available.

Lamin and the team were able to locate the place, and they conducted a search immediately. Seeds were indeed found in abundance. A few more teams with helicopters were sent to bring back the seeds. The problem of seed supply was resolved for the moment.

The seeds were processed instantly to meet the demand. The station was able to do that because of the high-tech equipment on-site. With sufficient manpower, the product could easily be manufactured in large quantities. The business was thriving again, and the foundation was happy with the whole situation.

The staff and workers were fully rewarded for a job well done. My research team was given an extra incentive of a holiday in the country of our choice. My wife and I went to the Bahamas in the Caribbean and spent a few weeks there.

The health product became popular and was accepted as a food supplement for health and vitality worldwide. The business for the product was thriving, and everyone reaped benefits from its sale. Some believed that the product would help them live longer. Due to its potency and quality, the product was increasingly in demand. This led to a profitable business for suppliers and distributors alike.

While production and supply were going well, the distributors suddenly began having problems with their cash flow. This was a result of the economic crisis all over the world. Due to this financial problem, many of the distributors closed down. Following that, they were unable to continue with their contracts.

This turn of events greatly affected our business. The foundation had to stop production and clear the stock. However, it was a little too late, and most of the stock could not be sold. The foundation was losing a lot of money, and drastic action had to be taken to save the foundation as a whole.

The foundation decided to confine its work on the island to research regarding the product. This had not been done earlier because they had not established a business foothold. As the business got bigger and the foundation exported the product to other countries, it was able to buy the land where the seed plants were found. This became a plantation area, and the research staff and workers were required to work at that location. The foundation knew that the economic downturn would not last long, and soon the whole business would be back on track.

True to their prediction, demand for the product returned, and distributors around the globe started placing orders. In no time, business was back to normal. The foundation was able to recoup its loss and once again profit from the product.

CHAPTER 14

In business, there is always competition. Another group of companies started to manufacture the same product on the Indonesian side of Borneo. They were able to gain a supply of the seeds at a location a few hundred kilometres from our plantation. Their plantation area was on the border between Malaysia and Indonesia.

They opened up an even bigger plantation than the foundation's, with research facilities and factories over the entire area. The owner was a multimillionaire businessman from Holland. He was able to buy and develop the area with the support of the Indonesian authorities. In return, the company employed many local people.

Initially, this business had a good relationship with the foundation. We exchanged visits and shared information regarding materials. We gained a lot through such cooperation and partnership.

The relationship turned sour as a result of an incident. One day, workers from the company were caught on foundation property by security guards. They were brought to the supervisor for interrogation.

'You were caught stealing our seeds. Do you admit that?' asked the supervisor.

'Yeah, we stole your seeds. What are you going to do?' they asked back.

'If it is true, we will send you to the security of our country. They will deal with you according to our law,' the supervisor replied.

'But we were told to steal your seeds,' they said.

'Who told you to do it?' the supervisor asked.

'Our boss,' they told him.

These workers were found stealing seeds from the stores at the plantation. When interrogated, they explained that they were encouraged to steal the seeds because our seeds were better than the ones found in their area. They were let go by the management, as this was their first offence.

The management of the Indonesian company denied that these workers were their employees. After that, there was tension between the company and the foundation whenever some minor incident happened.

This sour relationship became serious when more and more incidents of encroachment occurred. The workers of the Indonesian company informed us that there was not much work left at their plantation. Due to a bad harvest, the plantation was no longer producing as many seeds as before. The workers had been asked to find seeds outside the plantation itself, and so they went to the foundation plantation's side.

Discussions were held with the Indonesian company, but they didn't seem to take the matter seriously – until their workers were caught and finally sent to the Malaysian authorities. These workers were found guilty of trespassing as well as stealing seeds, and they were imprisoned for a couple of years. When the workers on the company's plantation learned about the case, they became angry and wanted the company to help them take revenge.

The company was in bad shape due to low production of seeds. Product sales were dwindling. They thought that by joining forces with the employees, they could do some damage to the foundation's reputation. So they agreed to let the workers launch an attack and equipped them with firearms and ammunition. When the workers reached the vicinity of the research station, the leader of the group, Bambang Sudorno, yelled, 'Everybody, let us go and attack!'

They all went to the same target – the main administration building – as they had not been properly instructed. When foundation security saw the armed group yelling and shouting a few hundred yards away, they alerted the rest of the security personnel. Although caught by surprise, the security force was ready to repulse an attack. The chief of security, Taha Budiman, said to his men, 'Get ready, and wait for my instruction.'

'Are we not going to go for them?' asked one of the security men.

'No. We are not sure how many there are. It's better to wait and see how they are attacking us, and then we fight back,' the chief said.

They waited for the attacking group to come closer. When the workers got close enough to the main administration building, they aimed and shot together like in a real battle. But the security force was able to defend the plantation, as they were well trained and well equipped with modern weaponry. Many of the local workers from the Dutch plantation died as a result of the gunfight. This only made the survivors more angry, and they were willing to go all out to fight for their fallen colleagues.

At first, the foundation did not want to involve the Malaysian authorities in the issue. So they tried to talk to the Indonesian authorities to resolve the problem. The government of Indonesia sent an official to calm the situation and contain the tension building up in the area. However, the locals were still not happy with the foundation management, because the management did not take action regarding the death of their fellow workers.

They made a secret arrangement to attack the foundation plantation again but on a larger scale. They gathered all the locals who had lost family members in the gunfight earlier, and they planned to launch a bigger assault with a few hundred volunteers. When the men were ready, they went to an area bordering the foundation plantation.

'We will attack them at dawn,' said the group's chief leader, Bambang Sudorno.

'How are we to attack them? They are well-equipped,' said one of the leaders.

'That's why we attack them by surprise,' Sudorno said.

However, the plan was leaked by one of the Indonesian workers employed by the foundation. So the foundation was in a state of readiness when the assault was made.

'*Serang*!' Sudorno yelled with his loud voice.

'*Tembak*!' the leaders of each group called out.

With more security and military personnel gathered, the foundation forces were ready to fight. The workers, with their outdated weapons, were no match. The number of casualties grew higher each day of their assault. But they persisted because they had the numbers.

The battle raged for days. The casualties were high, especially on the workers' side. Most of them could not stand the firepower of the foundation forces and died in their attempt to gain entry into the plantation. Some were caught and kept in a temporary lock-up.

The foundation forces suffered casualties as well. Most of those shot while defending their posts were employees from Indonesia. The research personnel were not directly involved. In fact, we were asked to stay at the research station while the fighting was going on.

Both the Malaysian and Indonesian authorities were informed of the conflict. They made attempts to stop the fight in order to save lives. Finally, Indonesian security forces were deployed to the area to stop the workers from further fighting. All those involved were detained and charged in court for starting the fight, including some from the plantation company management. Some were imprisoned, but those who were just following the orders of the leaders were set free.

After that, the plantation company stopped operating, as so many of the locals had died. The plantation was no longer supplying seeds for production. The management, which could not bear the cost of the incident, decided to close down.

The foundation went back to the way things were before the conflict. The business was progressing. With a sufficient supply of seeds, the products were being processed without problem to meet increasing demand from distributors. Business was booming again.

The foundation was happy with such good business. They were buying more land to develop more plantations. With the cooperation and close collaboration of the authorities, it seemed as though the future for the product was bright. The situation thus benefited the staff and workers as well as the country.

Once the business was in a strong position, the foundation's next step was to sustain the business. To do that, a promotional campaign was launched. I was sent to Moscow to promote the product in the Russian Federation with Zarrah Nur, my wife. I went there and established the network with the help of Andrew Philip, my old acquaintance.

The response from distributors in the Russian Federation was encouraging. I was able to penetrate even to the remote parts of the country. It was during my trip to the southern region that our team was ambushed by a rebel group in the area. We were brought to the camp to meet their leader. Together with my wife and three others, I was driven in a four-wheel-drive vehicle to a secluded part of the mountainous area.

'I am Yousef Baiyeb,' the leader said in introduction, shaking my hand. Wearing the full uniform of a soldier, he looked a full-fledged commander-in-chief – rather fierce-looking with his beard and moustache. His eyes nevertheless looked friendly.

'I am Mohd bin Zaidi,' I said.

'You are Muslim, right?' the leader asked.

'Yes, I am,' I answered.

'Where are you coming from?' he asked politely.

'We are from Malaysia,' I said.

'What are you doing in this part of the world?' he asked.

'We are promoting our product,' I answered.

'What product? Can we also buy it?' he asked with much interest.

'Our product is processed from seeds taken from the jungle. We have been selling it in many countries. It is designed to prolong human life,' I explained.

'If that is the case, we could also buy it for our men. They need such a product for our struggle,' he said.

'That would be good. Soon we will set up a distributing centre in Moscow,' I told him.

'All right. We will be glad to obtain the product from the centre,' he said. He then stopped talking and looked at the mountainside nearby. He looked sad and asked me, 'Have you heard about our struggle? We have been fighting for our freedom for decades. Many of our people have been killed,' he explained.

'I have followed your struggle and really sympathise with what your people have suffered,' I said.

'We would be very pleased if you could assist us in whatever way you can,' he begged.

I really was in sympathy with their plight and promised myself I would help them in whatever way I could with their struggle for freedom.

We were then allowed to go back to Moscow. However, on our way to the capital city, we were attacked by security forces from the government side.

'Let us go to the mountain,' yelled the leader into his walkie-talkie. There were three vehicles in the convoy.

'All right. We are following you,' yelled the rebels in the other two vehicles.

The government forces were in pursuit; however, the drivers knew the area well and were able to leave them behind.

Fortunately, we were saved by another rebel group that happened to be in the area, and they came to rescue us. We were again brought to the mountainous region to escape from the government attack.

Since we were with the rebels, we were being hunted by the government forces, and we had to hide in the mountainous terrain. The journey was tough, and sometimes we were unable to stop even for a rest. It was really difficult for my wife and me. The fighters were in high spirits. This could be due to their experience in warfare for decades.

Finally, we were able to get far away from the government forces. The place was quite safe due to the distance from government surveillance. The fighters were free to do their daily chores. The village was huge. There was a head man with a committee to administer the day-to-day communal activities.

My wife and I plus the two others were given a house to stay in. The rebels were not sure whether we should remain or be sent back to the capital. They were afraid that once the government knew that the rebels stayed in this village, they would be attacked with fighter jets.

We stayed in the village for about one month. The people were friendly and treated us well. We tried to help in whatever way we could with their daily activities. I was helping at a local school, teaching their children. My colleagues were helping the sick and those who needed medical treatment.

One day, I was able to communicate with the foundation through local radio communication and inform them of our predicament. They promised to get us out of the area through the Russian channels of authority. I cautioned them not to involve the government, lest they attack the place where we were being kept by the rebels.

After a while, I got a message from the foundation people that we would be allowed to go back to Moscow. Somehow, the foundation was able to get assistance from the local authorities to bring us out of the area through safe passage. After several days of walking, we were picked up by a convoy of vehicles from the foundation. We were lucky to be able to get out of the conflict area, or else we would be in the same situation as the film *Beyond Borders*, in which the lead character played by well-known film star Angelina Jolie was killed by rebel forces.

We were happy to be out of the area. However, I still felt that the rebel groups should be given the freedom they demanded. They just wanted to live in peace with others in their own country.

I remembered well the assurance of Yousef Baiyeb, the commander-in-chief, that they would buy the product. This could be another source of business, even though it might pose some problems. If they bought through middlemen, this could be a booming business.

Once in Moscow, we planned to establish a distribution centre for the product for the whole region. We could see there was a lot of potential in business expansion for the product here. Moreover, many Russians already lived longer lives. It would be easy for us to market a product meant to prolong human life.

After conducting an extensive survey of prospective customers, we found that the product was well received by the people at large. Following that, we decided to make Moscow the centre for product distribution for the whole region. We also appointed distributors in various cities and towns in the region. The business for the product was booming, and profits from the sale increased by leaps and bounds.

The foundation was very happy with the whole enterprise and decided to make Moscow the main distribution centre for the product in the northern hemisphere. However, after some time, competition arose from a local company that created a new product from ancient seeds. The ancient seeds were discovered in the northern region of Russia and were found to have ingredients that could sustain healthy living.

The ancient seeds were about two thousand years old and were recovered from excavations in the region by Russian scientists. The seeds were from fossils that were said to be 300 million years old. The scientists were able to reproduce them and then process them into a food supplement. The foundation found it difficult to compete with this new product. The Russian people changed their preference to their own company.

The foundation had to move the distribution centre out of Moscow. It was decided to make Amsterdam the centre. The foundation wanted another centre for the southern hemisphere. I was asked to search for a suitable place. After conducting several surveys to find prospective customers, it was decided to establish the distribution centre in Auckland, New Zealand. The product had been on the market throughout the country. It only needed to be expanded as per the demand and supply.

CHAPTER 15

New Zealand is not just a beautiful country where many tourists come and go. More importantly, the country remains untouched by urban development. It was a good move for the centre to be established in New Zealand, as the natives were closely associated with natural products, especially on North Island, where the country was still covered with forest and trees.

The Maoris were eager to do business, as the product could be sold throughout the country. They believed that the seeds were the legacy of their ancient ancestors, Patupaiarche, the mysterious forest-dwelling people or fairies of New Zealand.

They traced the origin of the seeds to the Malaysian jungle on the island of Borneo, from which they were brought to the Polynesian islands by the natives. The medicinal value of the seeds was found to be effective for all diseases. The seeds became the panacea for long life as told in local folklore.

The seeds grew naturally on the North Island of New Zealand. They were not only popular in New Zealand but also in most of the Polynesian islands. Fijians, Samoans, Tahitians, and Hawaiians also related the seeds to the local breeds. Due to the popularity of the seeds, the foundation business was well received by the people throughout the Polynesian islands.

I was invited to discuss a deal in Tahiti with the local businessmen. With a team, my wife and I went to the island by plane. When we arrived at the capital, Papeete, we were fascinated by the island's development and progress. With nostalgia, I recalled the story of the *Bounty*, which was about a mutiny when the crew captured the ship and set their captain, Bligh, in a boat in the middle of the ocean. The story of the mutineers was really interesting to recollect.

'I am a descendent of the mutineers,' said one businessman during our public discussion with the people of the island.

'A few of us settled on the island and began to develop it,' said another businessman.

'I can see that,' I said, as the development of the island was apparent.

Tahiti became a French protectorate after the natives were defeated in several wars with the Europeans. With the Europeans in charge, the islands were turned into a tourist paradise.

'How has this product come about?' asked one of the businessmen at the discussion.

I explained to the group about the research project undertaken by the foundation, the process of making the product, and the campaign to promote it around the world. After they got the information, they were impressed.

'How can we become distributors?' asked a local businessman.

'We could send our men here to help you start the business if you want. Since we've opened many distribution centres in many countries of the world, we could easily establish a network with those who are already doing well,' I told the group.

'That would be great,' said one of the local businessmen. As in Malaysia, the locals still needed assistance when it came to starting their businesses.

The businessmen finally agreed to sign a business contract with the foundation. They soon started their campaign to promote the product throughout the Tahitian islands. The response from the local people was very encouraging, and their business was doing well. The product became very popular.

The product was not only available at supermarkets, but also individual distributors were able to sell them in all parts of the country.

One day, I was invited by a group of local businessmen to come for a retreat at one of the islands. I went with Mr Lim and Lamin while my wife stayed at the capital, since it was a few-day event. We went by ship to the island; the ship belonged to one of the businessmen.

While on our journey, we were able to enjoy the scenery of the various islands we passed. Indeed, these were captivating and beautiful islands.

We arrived at our destination safely, and the three of us were given some time to provide sufficient information to those who took part in the event to be able to start their businesses. They were happy to be involved with the product, and they assured us that the product would get a good response from the population.

After that, we headed back to the main island on the ship we'd used previously. However, before we reached our destination, the ship's management was taken by surprise when the crew refused to continue the journey.

'We are asking for our rights. That's all,' said their leader, Mr Tiki Lefir, to the passengers who wanted to know why they refused to work.

'But don't you know that we, the passengers, will suffer if the ship does not go back?' Mr Tomlison Walter, a senior-citizen passenger, asked.

'We know that. But we are being treated badly and have asked many times for the management to resolve our request. So far, to no avail,' Mr Lefir said.

We were in the middle of the ocean. The captain refused to accede to the crew members' demand to solve their grievances. They wanted a better deal in terms of pay, perks, and privileges.

Because the captain was adamant, the crew continued the boycott. The ship was left unattended, and the passengers had to fend for themselves. We could not do much but leave the matter to the ship management.

The whole episode seemed to resemble what had happened to the *Bounty* many decades ago. We heard stories from the passengers that the crew really were not treated well. They could not bear to suffer such treatment any longer.

I was able to contact Zarrah Nur in the capital and relate the story of the ship's boycott. I told her not to worry, because the management was still in the mood to negotiate. Sooner or later, they would come to a settlement which would benefit both sides. The owner of the ship had been informed of the problem, and he was in favour of a suitable solution – that is, a win-win situation.

Finally, after a few days on the ocean, the crew agreed with the management's proposal. Everybody on the ship felt relieved and thanked the management and crew for their gentlemanly act of humanity.

We arrived at the capital to the joy of everybody, especially my wife. The businessmen were preparing for a grand get-together of all those involved with the product. They invited the local government leader to officiate, and invitations were extended to all the VIPs in the state capital. The event would mark the biggest reception for the product in the southern hemisphere.

On 1 November, the event unfolded with guests from all parts of the country. The spectacular reception was well attended, and the local government leader was happy to grace our gathering. The attendees were entertained by famous personalities, including internationally acclaimed singers and musicians. The event was a real success for the product, and its popularity soared to new heights.

After making sure the new venture was well established, we left Tahiti to go back to Auckland. The business in New Zealand was also thriving. Almost all the business outlets throughout the country reported a good turnover. We were all happy and hoped the business would remain strong against all odds and challenges.

My wife and I were content to spend most of our time in Auckland. We visited the outlets and at the same time did some charity work. For almost seven years, we had a good time and were regarded as respected citizens of the country. Although we were not yet permanent citizens, the recognition was given due to our charity work.

It was on one occasion of this charity work that I met Mr McNamara Jonathan, an influential Western business tycoon who proposed to buy the whole business. At first, I felt tempted by the proposal and agreed to discuss it further after consulting the board. However, when the board members heard about the proposal, they were surprised and dismayed. They thought that I was doing this in my own self-interest. Moreover, since I had been appointed as a board member after settling down in New Zealand, they thought it was unethical for me to make such a proposal. Without my consent, they decided to sack me from the board. I was, however, given all the perks and compensation for my contributions thus far.

Suddenly, I was left without any work to do. My colleagues were still with the foundation. It was a time of desperation; I wanted to start working again, and so I met another business tycoon from Japan. Mr Mori Yoji was one of those who had bargained to get their investment back when we promoted the product in Japan years earlier. He invited me to come to Japan and join his corporation, which dealt with pharmaceutical products. Without much hesitation, I grabbed the opportunity.

My wife and I moved to Japan, and we stayed in Tokyo. The corporation provided me with the facilities I needed. The corporation employed almost 100,000 people, had over 150 subsidiaries and affiliates throughout the country, and also had ten overseas plants. The current net sales on all their products came to over US $16 billion.

Being new in a big city, I spent a lot of time familiarising myself with my surroundings. After a few months, I adapted to the new work situation. The Japanese were friendly people to deal with, and they were always willing to give assistance when needed. They were known for their work ethics and hard work. Most of the time I was with the corporation, I was doing research and development. The staff was very helpful. They even had a place for children and wives to spend their time while their parents or husbands were at work. That way, staff were not worried about their families when they were required to stay late for work.

I was required to come up with the same seed product as that of the foundation. However, the new product was not made from natural-grown seeds but rather using bio-nano technology. After a few experiments, we were able to come up with a similar product and promote it for sale. The new product was very popular in Japan. Almost all pharmacy outlets were selling it.

The company's business surged, and it became well known throughout the country. The board decided to promote the health product to other countries. The response from overseas retailers was very encouraging, and the corporation was happy with the whole business. I was awarded with higher perks and privileges. I was all for the work with the corporation now.

There seemed to be a lot of opportunities for me in Japan. Some huge corporations made overtures to entice me to join them. However, I felt indebted to my current employer, as I had been sacked by the foundation and this corporation had welcomed me with open arms. Asian values were still very much in my blood to abort such temptation.

CHAPTER 16

The business world was fast-paced and challenging. My corporation faced internal conflict. The board members were no longer working together. This may have been a result of too much wealth generated by good business. The artificial seed products were really the jewel in the crown, and business was booming – so much so that the board members were no longer focusing on the big picture. They were making their own headway whenever opportunity arose. They all had their own personal agendas.

Historically, the Japanese were not very involved in business in the two hundred years of the Tokugawa era. Japan was a closed nation, with only the port of Nagasaki being used for trade with the Chinese and Dutch. The main reason for this isolation was to maintain the feudal system of the Tokugawa. It was in 1853 that Commodore Perry brought his black ship to Japan and demanded it open its doors to trade, spurring Japan's modern relations with the outside world. Within 135 years, Japan would become a centre of world trade and a major economic power.

The Japanese were fast learners, and once they involved themselves in any enterprise, they were bound to succeed. They were by nature very competitive, which sometimes was quite detrimental to their well-being and business. This is what was happening to the corporation once business was thriving. The board members started to go overboard.

Yakuza gangs became part of their business ventures, which included gambling, prostitution, and illegal trading. Board members would sometimes fight among themselves to get the business moving. This situation more often than not turned into fierce clashes between the groups supporting the board members. The gangs were more or less left to themselves to take care of their interests. This traced back to the yakuza tradition.

Since the business was not affected by such rivalry, I was not concerned by all that was happening around me. I cared more about the work entrusted to me by the corporation. Moreover, I really liked the environment, as well as the work ethic practised by the corporation staff. Even the environment outside was conducive to real human development. What a great country it was after such a historical blunder during the Second World War.

Thinking of what happened during the war, I couldn't imagine how such a civilized and humane people were once known to be cruel. During the war years, a lot of stories were told about atrocities in the territories under the control of Japanese soldiers. The people who came under Japanese occupation were not spared from harsh treatment, such as torture, rape, shootings, imprisonments, and group killings.

My village was no exception to the rule, and the people suffered. The country was destroyed. People lived in fear and under threats of all sorts. Many of the villagers became victims of the absolute autocratic regime. Some even ran and lived in the jungle just to save their lives. Those who remained under Japanese rule had to face cruelty and torture without end.

My grandmother said that the soldiers at first were well disciplined. But when they were drunk, they became animals, and they would go around the *kampong* (village) to search for women. They wouldn't care whether the women were married or not.

She told me a story of a young woman kidnapped by soldiers who happened to pass the village. This young woman, who lived with her grandmother, had just attained the age of puberty. She was so innocent, and to save her grandmother from being killed by the soldiers, she agreed to be the victim of the soldiers' dreadful lust. She had to deal with all the soldiers, and by the end, she succumbed to their brutal and inhuman acts and died.

The story became so well known that every generation after the war knew about it. The inhuman deeds of these Japanese soldiers were known to most Asian people. In South East Asia, the Chinese, Malays, Indonesians, Filipinos, and other natives were all subjected to the shameful acts of Japanese soldiers. Likewise, Koreans and mainland Chinese had dreadful stories to tell. The women who were sex slaves had become an issue between South Korea and Japan.

However, Japanese citizens of the modern independent nation had discarded what had happened in the past. As with any other nation involved in the world war, they regretted what the earlier generation did to the people who suffered during the war. In fact, they started a national policy of reconciliation right afterwards. They decided to become citizens of the civilised world like other advanced nations of the globe.

I was asked by the corporation to find an organiser for a so-called 'great debate' in which the new generation of youths throughout Japan were invited to take part. The topic of the debate was, 'Are Japanese Evil-Minded?' The focus was on the atrocities of the Japanese during their occupation of various parts of East Asia and South East Asia during the war. The corporation would sponsor the event. By doing that, the corporation was fulfilling its social corporate responsibility to inculcate good values in the younger generation.

The University of Tokyo agreed to be the organiser, with panellists from the top universities of Japan who were well versed in the history of the Second World War. They were educated and intellectual. What they said was very well articulated and based on facts. It was indeed enlightening to hear and see these panellists argue hard and sensitive issues with intellect and wisdom.

A debate of this kind was of great importance to the people of the world. They could share what had happened in the past. They could also be enlightened by the actual facts and figures, which they then could rationalise. Thus, people would really know what had happened and judge for themselves.

The corporation believed that the new generation could become national ambassadors. When dealing with a booming business, it was appropriate to enlighten the new generation about what had happened in the past.

The debate was well received by the audience, who were mostly the youths of Japan. They were polite and followed the session throughout without any untoward behaviour. The panel took turns arguing the topic with an independent moderator, Professor Lee Chong Soon, who was from a well-known university in Singapore. Let us follow some of the deliberation from this great debate:

> **Professor Lee:** This is a special event organised mainly for the youths of Japan. You must be aware of what has taken place on the world stage which involves your country. Even though the event has taken place a long time ago, it is good to learn from history to ensure the mistakes made are not repeated. Without much ado, I would like to invite the first speaker to make his argument.
>
> **Mr Abe Hashimoto:** Thank you. This is indeed a special event, and I would like to thank the organiser for being able to come up with the idea of having this debate. I am sure the debate will be of benefit not only to the youths but also to the people of Japan by and large.
>
> My first point would be to explain why the Japanese did such things during the war. As we all know, whenever there is a conflict, we cannot possibly control some of those involved from doing bad things. There are many examples of brutality either during the big war or between countries or within such countries. However, the point we need to be aware of is who were the people behind such brutal acts and what do we need to do with them.
>
> In the case of Japanese atrocities during the war, those who were directly responsible were the soldiers and not the Japanese civilians. Thus, after the war, these soldiers were found

guilty of the acts and severely punished. Therefore, those who were responsible have been dealt with. Now, the Japanese people are always reminded of the tragic event and they are more enlightened.

Secondly, the Japanese were by nature not aggressive. However, due to the war, they were required to defend as well as extend their national territory; the soldiers in particular were just following orders from the higher-ups. They fought the war against formidable enemies, namely the Allied Forces, courageously. This could be seen in a film called *Windtalkers* with the famous actor Nicholas Cage who was killed in the battle in the film. Another film called *The Thin Red Line* also shows the raging battle between the Japanese forces and the Americans. The battle took place in the Solomon Islands. From these films, we could say that the Japanese who fought courageously against their enemies were mainly following orders from the higher-ups. Thus, they were forced to do what they were instructed to do for the sake of their country's honour.

Professor Lee: Now let us hear from the second speaker.

Mr Harukami Saito: Thanks for inviting me to take part in this special debate. I guess the idea behind this great debate is no doubt to enlighten the youths of what happened in the war in which Japan was involved. It was something of a human tragedy when war turned the country into a war zone. The battlefield, in particular, was ravaged to the ground because the opposing forces tried to beat the others. The worst thing that happened was no doubt to the people caught in between. Human lives were no longer of any value to the forces at war. They could not differentiate whether to kill or not. This is because they had to defeat their enemies come what may. Therefore, there is nothing to gain from war. The people of the world should reject violence towards humanity.

The great debate continued with questions from the audience. There were arguments and counter arguments.

One audience member was not in agreement with most of what had been said by the speakers. 'In my opinion, the Japanese did have the ambition to become a great power,' he said. 'That's why before the Second World War, they were already aggressively extending Japan's national territory – beginning in 1931 with the invasion of Manchuria and continuing in 1937 with the invasion of China. To say that the extension of the war to the south-east region was due to the Second World War is not really correct. It seems it was due to their ambition to become a great world power like Germany and Italy.'

Another audience member took up the argument. 'I agree – the Japanese had an ambition to become a great power. Otherwise, they would not have invaded Manchuria and China, or extended their quest for national territory to the other regions. In fact, they formed an axis with Germany and Italy so that they could conquer the world.'

Another audience member added, 'Of course, during the war we could not possibly ensure that atrocities wouldn't happen. But the fact remains that if the war had not been started, such atrocities may not have occurred. Therefore, the onus is still on the warring faction.'

The debate ended with everybody being enlightened regarding the bad outcome of the war. The debate also provided great publicity for the corporation sponsoring it. It was aired on several main Japanese TV channels, including NHK WORLD, and was watched not only by the people of Japan but worldwide. The debate was conducted professionally, just like the well-known great debate organised by Al Jazeera in Doha, Dubai.

CHAPTER 17

After the event, the corporation became better known throughout the world. This really helped to project the image of the corporation and its business. The product was in tremendous demand. It became so profitable that it made the corporation one of the leading business powerhouses.

As always happens in the business world, success breeds rivalry. Business as such generates competition between groups as each one tries to overcome the others. In the case of this corporation, the rivalry was between the influential board members.

One group was led by Mr Mori Yoji, the chairman of the board. He seemed to command the majority of the members, as he was the founder of the company. He was liked by many, and because of him the corporation was doing very well. He was also respected by the community at large and was doing a lot of charity work. In business circles, he was regarded as a leading figure. He would easily be able to gain the people's support if he ran for political office.

Another group followed Mr Tsuji Yuji, a leading figure who was making headlines as the most influential businessman. He was a smart and cunning business baron. It was said that he was a member of Yatagarasu or Three-Legged Crow, an ancient Japanese secret society based in

Kyoto that originated from ancient tradition. Legend had it that a crow with three legs guided the first inhabitants to the Japanese archipelago. For this reason, the three-legged crow was an important symbol in ancient Japanese Shinto.

Mr Yuji was one of the leaders of this secret society. Thus, he was able to order the yakuza gangsters to do whatever he wanted. Even though he was not supported by many of the board members, he could always do something to force them to come to his side. Thus, there was always intense competition between the two groups.

These competitions between board members had been ongoing for quite some time. Now, it had become more intense as the two leaders gathered their influences. However, as normally happens in the corporate world, competition took place more between the associates or underlings. The leaders, especially at the top, were not directly involved. Those in the lower ranks tried to outperform each other to get the leaders' blessing and recognition.

With the competition so intense, the two leaders gradually became involved more directly. During one of the board meetings, the two argued angrily.

'You shouldn't involve criminals in this organisation,' Mr Yoji told Mr Yuji.

'What do you mean?' asked Mr Yuji.

'Your yakuza gangs are harassing my men,' Mr Yoji replied.

'Are you accusing me? I don't involve yakuza gangs! How come you said that?' asked Mr Yuji.

'I have proof that you are involved!' insisted Mr Yoji.

'Show me the proof, if you really have it,' challenged Mr Yuji.

'That's your character, always deny when you do bad things,' Mr Yoji said, raising his voice.

'It's not true unless you can prove it. I don't involve criminals in our organisation,' Mr Yuji shouted back.

'You should be ashamed!' Mr Yoji said angrily.

They stood up from their chairs. Mr Yuji went to the front where the chairman was, and they started punching each other. The other board members were quick to stop them before any serious incident happened.

The final straw that broke the camel's back came when Mr Yoji's grandson was kidnapped by the other group's gang members. This really incensed the business tycoon and led to war between the two groups.

When Mr Yoji learned of his grandson's kidnapping, he summoned all of his associates and underlings to a meeting place. Mr Yoji himself chaired the gathering.

'I would like to inform all of you that I will not tolerate such an unbecoming act!' he roared, expressing his anger towards the group that had kidnapped his grandson. Everyone present was quiet and sympathised with him. Every person expressed sympathy for the chairman.

'Yes! Yes! We support you, honourable sir,' the audience responded.

'I need you to commit to our group pledge that if one of us is being intimidated and victimised, all of us without exception have to act – and act decisively, for the good of all,' he reminded those present.

'Yes! Yes! Yes! We agree, honourable sir,' they replied in unison.

'My grandson has been kidnapped. Next time it could be a member of your family,' he continued.

'Yes! Yes! Yes! We sympathise and share your grief,' they again responded loudly.

'Are all of you ready to act to bring back my grandson?' he asked the audience.

'Yes! Yes! Yes, honourable sir! We will bring back your grandson to you!' they replied with a loud voice in unison.

'What will you do?' he asked with a commanding voice.

'We will search all corners of the country,' they responded again with an even louder voice.

'How long will it take you to do this?' he asked, wanting to get their assurance.

'Give us a couple of days! We will succeed in our effort!' they responded loudly, with confidence.

'All right! I place my confidence in all of you to do so.' He gave a go-ahead to do what they had said.

With that, the meeting ended. Apart from the general staff, those who attended the gathering were board members. Almost all the board members were present except Mr Yuji and a few of the board members who supported him.

The search for the chairman's grandson was initiated immediately. All the various branches of the corporation throughout the country were informed of the matter. Each branch then had its task force trying to find information regarding the whereabouts of the boy. Once they located the victim, they were to inform HQ before taking further action. Of course, all this was done discreetly in order to keep from tipping off the other group.

Nevertheless, the other group was aware of the whole operation. This no doubt complicated matters, as they could outmanoeuvre the rescuers.

Each group used gangs to carry out their mission. More often than not, these gangs were vicious in their execution. They were driven by the promise of huge prizes if they were successful. They would kill or be killed.

After several days, the gangs working for the chairman's group were able to locate his grandson. The head of the group gave an order to surround the place. 'When I give the order, only then do you attack,' he reminded his men. They moved cautiously towards the building. There were several guards on duty, with a couple more inside the building.

'All right – two of you go and get the guards at the front door,' the head gave the order. Two men with careful step went to the front door and overtook the guards. The head then signalled the rest to go inside the building.

The kidnappers were not aware of the intended assault and were taken by surprise. There was a fierce gunfight between the two groups. Finally, the chairman's group was able to defeat the other group. The boy was brought to his parents, and his grandfather was happy with the outcome of his underlings' efforts. They were all fully rewarded.

The other group was now even more furious and full of vengeance. They would leave no stone unturned to take revenge, as they had lost face. In Asian culture, to lose face was like a death penalty.

CHAPTER 18

After the chairman's grandson was rescued, Mr Yuji was furious with his men for not being able to prevent the other group from getting the boy. I was told about this by one of the board members. Mr Yuji declared an open war on the other group and gave orders to 'capture this guy with all our might'. My photo was then distributed to all the yakuza gangsters.

I was involved in this rivalry due to my close association with the chairman. He was the one who had offered me the job when I was sacked by the foundation. The other group's leader was mad at me because of several decisions made by the board. He was always on the losing side when the board made big business decisions. I was not involved in the decision-making, but the chairman was known to consult certain people before making important decisions, and I was one of them. More often than not, my ideas and suggestions were the ones being considered, and the leader of the other group couldn't accept that. Thus, he regarded me as an enemy, as most of his proposals were rejected by the board.

The gang directed by that leader became more brutal in its attempt to capture me. Fortunately, the corporation dedicated itself to ensuring my safety. This was another great Asian value – loyalty to the chairman who entrusted them with responsibility. I was given protection by the corporation, and the men followed the directive to make my safety their top priority.

With the strength of the yakuza group under Mr Yuji, there was no doubt that it was going to be difficult for the chairman's group to keep me safe. The yakuza was well known in Japan, even though they were not regarded as a threat to society. Their numbers were equal to half of the workforce numbers of the Japanese Self-Defence Forces, commonly called *Jieitai*.

The yakuza were involved in criminal acts, but they did them subtly. Sometimes they were referred to as a *boryokudan* or *gokudo* or 'violent group'. But they preferred to call themselves a *ninkyo dontai* or 'chivalrous group', as they did help with search and rescue and disaster relief work whenever there were natural disasters.

Using the raw public numbers of yakuza members, they could be regarded as the largest criminal organization in the world. They had offices, or at least 'representatives', in any town with more than a hundred thousand citizens. Their members could be found all over the country.

There was no doubt they would be able to locate me whenever I moved around. This time, their aim was nothing less than to go for a kill. I was back in Tokyo after moving around the country. The corporation was able to find a place for me and my wife which was thought to be safe. I stayed in an apartment with tight security.

However, the other group was tipped off by some of the people inside. I found myself vulnerable and an easy target. One fatal weekend when I was eating dinner in the apartment, they made a move.

They came with a helicopter and were hovering around when the phone near the front door rang. I took the call and was informed I had urgent mail that needed to be collected immediately. The man introduced himself and by his voice I believed that he was the postman. I went down to the lobby, and it was then that the hovering helicopter began shooting at our apartment. After several rounds of firing, they left the place. One of the bodyguards was shot dead; another was able to escape and came down to inform me. He and another two guards from the lobby rushed me to a car stationed nearby and sped away.

'What a close call!' said the chief bodyguard.

'What was that all about?' I asked, not knowing what had happened.

'They shot at your apartment. Possibly they thought you were in there!' he explained.

'Really! My goodness! It was fate then that the postman called me to get the mail. Had that call not been made, I would have still been in the apartment. I would dead!' I said gratefully. It was also a blessing that my wife was off shopping at a nearby supermarket at the time.

We fetched my wife at the supermarket and drove to another location. The place was quite secluded, and this time, we stayed in a bungalow. The house was well equipped, especially in terms of security. The corporation really made sure that this time my wife and I were safe. I still had unfinished work with the corporation, and the chairman already had a plan for me to move out of the country.

We were not allowed to go out as freely as before. This was to avoid being detected by the other gang group. Whenever we wanted to go out, there had to be security men around. On a number of occasions, we were being followed.

One day, I talked to the chief guard, as my wife and I wanted to visit some famous and popular places in Japan. After the discussion, we decided to visit several places at one go. This was to avoid too much exposure and hinder detection by the other group members.

First we visited the former samurai districts, namely Tokyo, Osaka, and Nagoya. The tourist guide explained to us about the places we visited: 'In the Edo era, the three districts of Tokyo, Osaka, and Nagoya were developed into castle towns. The local feudal lords resided in the centrally located castles.' We followed the crowd going around one of the castles in the Tokyo district.

The guide continued, talking into her loudspeaker, 'The feudal lord had the samurai to guard him. The samurai lived in the district surrounding the castle.' We were walking along a lane lined with the white walls and wooden gates of a former samurai mansion. The mansion was preserved as heritage. Some houses in the district were open to the public.

Next, we were brought to the imperial palace, located in the middle of Tokyo. The palace was not open to the public, only the imperial gardens. We went to the gardens and were shown the stadium and museum. It was while we were in the Kitanomaru Garden that the other group members suddenly appeared.

They got hold of my wife and me and took us to a vehicle not far from the garden. However, our security men were able to intercept the vehicle. There was a gunfight between the two groups, and we were able to run away from the scene with the help of our chief guard and two of his assistants. As we fled the area, the other group members were in hot pursuit. But our security men were more efficient, and we were able to leave the area safely.

From information gathered by our security men, it seemed that the other group had changed its earlier objective. Instead of aiming to kill me, now they wanted me alive. They had realised that I could be an asset for them; they might be able to persuade me to join their group.

The following day, we went from Tokyo to Kyoto. It was interesting to note that the Japanese people were so cultured. They greeted us politely when we visited the shopping complexes and even the ordinary shops. Their dances and festivals were also a reflection of their culture. We could see this cultural aspect of the Japanese from the artefacts and showcase materials exhibited in their museums.

While we walked along the rows of shops at the city centre, suddenly a black E250 Mercedes stopped just at the side of the road. A few hefty-looking men came straight for us and forced us to enter the car. One of them pointed a gun at us and indicated that we should follow immediately. We had no choice but to comply.

Once our security men realised we had been abducted by the gang, they ran towards the car. But the gang was already in the car and immediately left the place. Our security men ran quickly to their vehicle and chased us. It was a horrifying experience when the gang drove the car at high speed, followed by our security men. It took several hours, but our security men were able to outmanoeuvre our captors.

The gang members were caught red-handed by our security men. There was a gunfight, but our security men overpowered them. They ran away, leaving me and my wife in their car. How grateful my wife and I were to our security men!

We moved on to yet another apartment which was quite far away from the city centre – but still, our whereabouts was detected by the other group. It was surprising sometimes how that group was able to locate us. One day while we were shopping in the village, suddenly there was a car with four people inside, following us wherever we went. Our bodyguards were quick to act, leading us behind the shop through a back door so we could leave the area unnoticed by the group. This happened several times.

Eventually we seldom moved around, staying at home most of the time. This was also not helping much. On one occasion, while we were having dinner at home, the telephone began to ring. Thinking that the call was from our children back home, I picked up the phone.

'Hello, Mr Zaidi is speaking!' I said.

There was silence for quite a while. No reply from the other side.

'Hello. Who is calling?' I spoke again.

Still silence. I put down the phone, but it rang again.

'Hello. Hello. Who is calling?' I repeated several times. But there was no reply. Finally I decided not to pick up the phone when it kept ringing. Sure enough, it was discovered that the call was made by the gang. This was confirmed by our chief bodyguard. He told us not to use the phone anymore. From then on, we used a mobile phone.

Since the gang had located us, we moved again – this time, back to the city centre. The place was quite exclusive, and we assumed that we wouldn't be followed this time. My wife and I tried to live normal lives. We went to shop at uptown shopping complexes and enjoyed our new freedom. For quite a while, we lived undisturbed, and we treasured this life of affluence.

As we started to adjust ourselves to the neighbourhood and mix with the locals, however, we were confronted by a local gang. In fact, they were not yakuza, just a gang that was into local activities of extortion and intimidation.

While we were doing some shopping at a local shop, this group came at us suddenly. Two of them forced us to go to the corner.

'We want money! Money!' one of them said.

'Don't have much money,' I replied.

'Give us your wallet! Wallet!' one of them demanded.

Once they got the wallet and saw that there was not much money in it, they ordered us to follow them to a car outside the shop. Fortunately, our security men saw what was going on – and once the gang realised we had security men, they quickly ran away. Our chief of security immediately came to our aid, and we were taken away from the area.

CHAPTER 19

The corporation had just embarked on a new project to produce a supplement for export. I was needed to ensure that the project went through. I was being held on to until the project was successfully implemented. However, I was facing a dilemma. Since we had been subjected to incident after incident, we were living in fear. My wife and I had to be guarded round the clock.

Life as fugitives was no longer tenable for me and my wife. Apart from our lives being in danger, what was worst was that we were like running dogs being chased from one place to another. As the other group had members all over the country, there was no place for us to hide anymore.

In order to deceive the gangs, our security people chose a neighbourhood in a prefecture where a particularly violent faction of the yakuza operated. It was a rust-belt region on the southernmost island of Japan and had the largest number of organized crime groups in the country. They were involved in so-called 'business interests', including prostitution, real estate, stockbroking, moneylending, and so on.

There was constant infighting as well as open wars between the factions. Some of them were not petty criminals confined to the streets; they were international businessmen using knowledge, money, power of persuasion, and influence with the government to secure their lucrative international black business deals.

The authorities were unable to deal with these gangs decisively due to their cunning acts. This was mainly because they had connections within law enforcement who were willing to help them. Moreover, to the ordinary citizen, they appeared polite, well-mannered, and no threat at all. But if you were to do business with them, make no mistake, they were ruthless, calculating people who would not hesitate to better their position at the cost of their rivals.

We had no other choice but to make a life decision. We had been happy to work and live in Japan. I had learnt a lot about Japanese values, either related to work or to life in general. Indeed, we really didn't want to leave Japan. But after considering all of the options available, we finally had to discuss our predicament with the corporation. The corporation as always was quite sympathetic.

When the going got tough, a decision was made that I must go somewhere else. The corporation finally allowed me to go to another country. It took quite some time for them to let me go, as my expertise was required to complete the new supplement.

I was forced to leave Japan to escape the gangs' constant threats. There was no way for the corporation to come to an amicable compromise between the rival groups. In fact, the rivalry was only becoming more intense, and the clashes were becoming much more open.

The corporation decided I should go to British Columbia, Canada. At first, I was keen to go to Hong Kong or Macau, which were near to my country. But the corporation felt it would be safer for me and my wife to be in a non-Asian country, and we agreed.

Without official notification of the board members, I was flown to Vancouver. We hoped that the yakuza would let me live in peace, as I was no longer in Japan. However, we were wrong. The gangs were still trying to get me.

At first, I didn't realized why the other group would be so determined to capture me. When I checked my possessions, I realized it was the original formula to produce artificial seeds that they were after. I was the only one who had it in my possession besides the chairman of the board. Moreover, we were also the only persons who knew the processing and production of the seeds in the original form – when we first met, I explained it to him. Just by having me, they could easily continue producing the seeds without the board's approval.

Knowing that I was behind the corporation's success and well aware of their reliance on me, I did something unethical. This was partly because I was considering quitting my job. I could no longer stand being the target of the other group. If the corporation went bust, there was a chance that I could stop working with them.

The current formula and processing of the seeds was not being done according to the original plans. Therefore, the supplement was not as good as before. The public realised that the supplement was a fake and decided to stop buying. The corporation was losing a lot of money, but there was not much they could do about it. They thought that this was a normal phenomenon in the business world.

I believed that natural seeds were more effective than artificial ones. There was a comparative study done in China that showed this to be true. Even Professor Wong from Peking University, Beijing had mentioned the effectiveness of natural seeds over artificial ones.

I wanted the corporation to do what the foundation did: go to the island where the seeds were found, plant the seeds, and process them into supplements for sale. There might be competition, but if it was done well, they needn't be worried.

The rainforest where the seeds were available was still intact. The island was still covered by forest and jungle where indigenous tribes lived. In fact, they could easily obtain permission to start a business, since the country was in need of foreign investment. They refused to do that, as the cost was huge. They insisted on continuing with the production of the artificial seeds.

CHAPTER 20

After we were targeted several more times, the corporation decided to bring my wife and me to Vancouver Island. They had prepared a boat, the *Lucky While*, and made a plan to keep the yakuza from knowing we were no longer on the mainland. The corporation knew that even in Vancouver, there were yakuza. Our security men were quite prepared to face the challenge.

The boat had a high-powered engine with a radar system and all the necessary communication gadgets. There was also a small boat, like a dinghy, which could be used in case the bigger boat faced problems. The small boat was also equipped with a high-powered engine. The corporation wanted to make sure that my wife and I were safe and fully guarded for any eventuality.

On the scheduled date, we left Vancouver and travelled to the designated place. The chief guard had given instructions to his men on what to do in order to deceive the other gang.

'We will go by two cars to the designated place,' the chief guard explained.

'How long for us to make a ploy in order for the other group to be unaware of our move?' asked one of the guards.

'We will communicate with you as we go to several places,' the chief guard said.

'All right. We will follow whatever instructions you give us,' said the other guards.

We hoped that the gang wouldn't know we were leaving for another place. Our entourage of seven people left our hiding place using separate vehicles. This was again to avoid being detected by the gang members.

The group that protected my wife and I took a longer route. We went to the northern part of the country before going to the city centre and the place where the boat was waiting. There was nothing for us to worry about, as everything was well planned by the chief bodyguard.

As we drove towards the city on our way from the north, suddenly we were being followed by a black vehicle – a Mercedes S350 series – as we passed the Marine Drive from Patterson.

'You see that car? They already detected us,' the chief guard told the driver.

'What we do now?' asked the driver.

'Just drive on and find a way to outmanoeuvre them,' replied the chief guard.

Our vehicle continued on the usual roads, passing the Boundary Road to the River District, and then went straight towards Highway 1. But then we drove to Richmond and waited there for a while to ensure that the other car had lost us.

At first, we didn't realise that we were being followed, as there was nothing suspicious about the vehicle. But when after every turn we made the car was still tailing us, we knew it was after us. The driver drove faster and faster, trying to leave Richmond County through inner roads. We came back to Highway 1, drove to Surrey, and waited there for a while. From there we went back to Burnaby by inner roads and went to Kingsway. It was from there that we drove to the city centre.

Once we reached the city centre, the driver drove the car through the back lanes and finally came to Glanville Island, where the boat was waiting. The other car also came.

'Now we go to the boat. Quickly!' the chief guard informed everybody.

'How about our cars?' asked the drivers.

'We can leave them here. But one driver needs to stay back to let us know if the gang members came after us,' said the chief guard.

'I would like to join you!' said the driver who was with the other car. He looked a bit sinister and serious looking.

'All right, you can come with us,' said the chief guard. The driver smiled, and his face was full of joy.

Without wasting much time, we went straight to the boat and left the place immediately. The pursuing car with its passengers was nowhere to be seen, and we assumed they were unable to detect our whereabouts. However, not long after that, that car came to Glanville Island also. The gang members went to their boat and sped up out of the jetty. The driver immediately informed the chief guard.

Our boat was heading towards Vancouver Island when the other boat appeared, going out towards the sea. We thought it was just an ordinary boat. Our prediction was wrong; the boat was, in fact, following us at a distance. When our people realised that, the chief guard instructed the driver to go in the direction of Campbell River.

Upon reaching the mouth of the river, instead of going up, the driver turned toward Quadra Island and proceeded to the Discovery Islands. Because of the many small islands there, our boat was able to leave the pursuing boat far behind. However, once we came out from the small islands, the other boat was able to catch up. The boat seemed to be faster than ours.

The pursuing boat was getting closer. It was using a high-powered engine and coming very fast. From a distance, we could see the gang members ready to make an attack with their machine guns. The boat was running at full speed, as seen by the waves created as they advanced towards us.

At about three hundred metres away, they started to shoot incessantly. Our boat was still fast-running and leaving them a bit behind. Then our boat engine abruptly stopped. The boat driver tried to start and restart the engine, but to no avail. We had to make a decision fast, without wasting any time.

The chief guard ordered the driver to get the dinghy ready and lower it into the water. The three of us – myself, my wife, and the driver – boarded the dinghy in a hurry. We then sped off to the nearest island, leaving the chief guard and the four others on board.

The pursuing boat was gaining on our boat. They started shooting again and getting closer. Suddenly, our boat burst into flames, followed by a big explosion. We witnessed this incident from the island where we were hiding.

As we came out from that island, another big boat suddenly appeared. The people on board gave a signal for us to stop. To my surprise, the driver followed what the person in the other boat wanted. As the other boat approached ours, I could see who was in it. Mr Tsuji Yuji was there, and he was smiling at us.

'How are you, Mr Zaidi?' he greeted me from a distance. Our dinghy came closer to the other boat, and we were asked to come aboard.

'Fine, Mr Yuji,' I said after we were on his boat.

'I am happy that you are safe,' Mr Yuji said with a smile.

'Thanks, Mr Yuji,' I said, and he continued talking. He was proposing that I should work with his group. He was in favour of my suggestion that the corporation venture into the natural seeds business.

'How about my job in the corporation?' I asked.

'We can use this incident to cover up your whereabouts.' He said that he would let me and my wife go free, and he would persuade the board members to agree with the proposal and let me take charge of the business on Borneo.

When we arrived at Glanville Island, he asked if I would accept the offer. Before we parted, he handed me a parcel with two items written on the cover. One was free accommodations in a five-star hotel for me and my wife while we were in Vancouver, and the other was the business offer for Borneo.

He again pleaded with me to accept the offer. 'Please consider the offer for your good self and intellectual wisdom,' he reminded before he left us, followed by his men. My wife and I went to the Fairmont Empress Hotel to check in. Once in the hotel, I went through the business offer thoroughly.

It was indeed an especially good offer, and thus I had a dilemma: to accept or not to accept. If I accepted, then I was free to go back home to Malaysia and start the new business venture. If not, I might face the wrath of Mr Yuji and his gang. After a long and deliberate soul-searching, I finally made up my mind: I accepted the offer.

The following day, the boat incident was reported on in two mainstream newspapers, the *Vancouver Sun* and the *Vancouver Province*, and on the TV news. It was said that the boat was broken into pieces and that there was no sign of survivors.

Printed in the United States
By Bookmasters